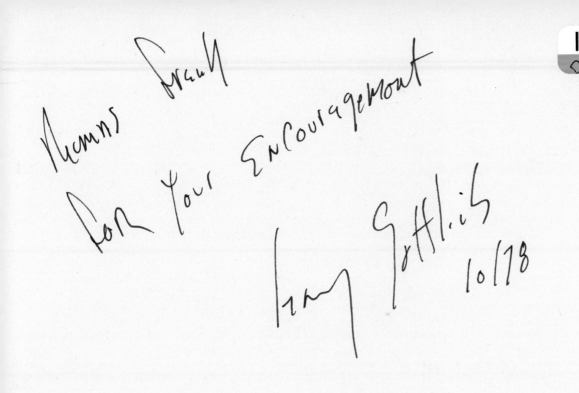

Thanks Frank
For Your Encouragement

Irwin Gottlieb
10/78

FACTORY MADE

FACTORY MADE

HOW THINGS ARE MANUFACTURED

Written by Leonard Gottlieb with photographs by the author

HOUGHTON MIFFLIN COMPANY BOSTON 1978

I mean to put a potato into a pillbox, a pumpkin into a tablespoon,
the biggest sort of watermelon into a saucer.
The Turks made acres of roses into attar of roses,
I intend to make attar of everything. . . .

GAIL BORDEN
Inventor of Condensed Milk

Library of Congress Cataloging in Publication Data

Gottlieb, Leonard.
  Factory made.

  1. Manufacturing processes—Juvenile literature.
I. Title.
TS183.G67   670   78-18007
ISBN 0-395-26450-2

A 10 9 8 7 6 5 4 3 2 1

For My Parents

CONTENTS

Toilet Seats   1

Baseballs   8

Buttons   15

Fire Hydrants   23

Paintbrushes   34

Matches   42

Rubber Bands   50

Nails   58

Plastic Bottles   66

Foam Rubber   73

Bricks   82

Asphalt Concrete   94

Eyeglass Frames   104

INTRODUCTION

Recently I visited a factory that was die-cutting rolls of adhesive-backed printed labels. The rolls were being cut into two million quarter-inch sections by an expensive and sophisticated automatic die-cutting machine. The labels were instructions on how to put up a wall-mounted holding fixture to hang sets of plastic measuring cups.

Two million sets of measuring cups! Although the housewares company that distributes them is rather large, it is only one out of potentially hundreds that manufacture and distribute this product. How many measuring cups are manufactured in this country in one year? The number must be enormous. Are they being hoarded? Should I buy futures? The ancient Romans believed in minor deities for household objects. If these deities still exist and the one for measuring cups decided to gather all American measuring cups in one place—what structure should be rented that would be large enough to contain them?

If our knowledge of primitive and ancient cultures is largely based upon the discovery and analysis of their tools and artifacts, then some of these measuring cups will be the objects by which our culture will be known in the future. The products examined in this book are also the symbols of our civilization. They are the materials and goods that in many ways are the "stuff" of our daily lives.

Some of the products are the result of the distillation of hundreds of years of tradition and craft filtered through modern cost and efficiency analysis. Other products have evolved from the revolution in petroleum technology, primarily since the Second World War.

The firms visited ranged from a small family partnership (buttons) to a division of a multi-national billion dollar corporation (bottles); from an old firm full of tradition that has made the same product at the same location using machinery more than a hundred years old (bricks) to a company that is on the crest of the fashion wave, sensitive to the slightest nuances of consumerism (eyeglass frames).

When I first started visiting factories I was impressed with the image that these were places most people knew little about. I thought the standardization of products, specialization of jobs, the phenomenal volumes of materials, and the exotic machinery were all part of a world kept hidden behind the anonymous walls of factories.

Ten years and hundreds of factories later, it has become apparent that these concepts have merged into the public view and have become accepted as the measures of effectiveness. The quick visit to one of the famous fast food palaces is a succinct introduction to many of these basics of factory methodology: the division of labor, the replacement of skill with detail work, the concentration of technical knowledge in non-production employees, the utilization of "cheap labor," and, finally, the mass production of a product which has become almost a necessity of modern life.

LEONARD GOTTLIEB

FACTORY MADE

TOILET SEATS

In 1975 less than 1 million new housing units were constructed, but in the same year the American toilet seat industry produced 18 million seat and cover combinations. The average firm produced 4 million in twenty different models and thirty-five colors.

Toilet seats can be made by a thermoplastic injection molding machine, using plastic pellets, or in a thermosetting molding press, using a mixture of wood flour and plastic resin.

Thermoplastic materials are processed to produce a *physical* change, either in shape, texture, or density. Thermoplastic materials can be likened to ice cubes, which can be melted into water and refrozen into cubes or other shapes. *Thermosetting* materials undergo a *chemical* change, which produces a material basically different in form than its ingredients. When an egg is boiled, it undergoes a permanent change of its chemical as well as its physical structure.

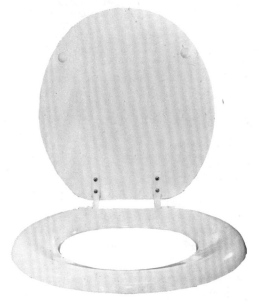

Plastic seats

Only a quarter of the toilet seats made are of the more expensive impact-resistant polystyrene. These are made by a screw injection molding machine, which can produce a molded seat and cover every five minutes. Polystyrene pellets are fed into the machine through a hopper. The machine melts six and a half pounds of pellets, the amount

This hydraulic screw injection molding machine is used to make plastic toilet seats. A worker stands in front of the hopper containing the polystyrene pellets. The molds are behind the sliding doors to the worker's left.

needed to make a seat and cover, at 400° F, and forces, or injects, it at 10,000 pounds per square inch (psi) pressure into a chrome-plated mold.

The mold, which costs $80,000, consists of two halves of machined die steel. Each section has half of the shape of the seat machined out of its center. When the mold is closed, a cavity is formed in the middle that is the exact shape of the seat and cover. The mold has internal runner and channel systems, which allow the melted plastic and water to enter the mold. To prevent the plastic from leaking out of the joined halves of the mold, 1200 tons of clamping pressure are exerted by a powerful hydraulic system.

After the melted plastic has been injected through the runner system into the cavity of the mold, it begins to solidify. Cool water is then run into a separate channel system built into the mold to quicken the cooling process. The mold is then separated, and the operator removes the seat

The two-part mold for the toilet seat and cover. When it is closed, a cavity is formed in the exact shape of the seat and cover. In the middle of the narrow channel between the lid and the seat, precisely in the center of the right half of the mold, is a small hole. The melted plastic is forced into the mold through this hole. In the corresponding place in the left half of the mold, a cooled piece of plastic protrudes outward. Perpendicular to this protrusion are two other hardened plastic rods. These pieces indicate the route the melted plastic follows to fill the mold cavities.

and cover, breaks off the chunk of plastic that formed within the runner system, and places the seat and cover in a cool water bath. Because it is a thermoplastic product, the seat could conceivably be ground up into pellets and the process could be repeated with the same result.

While the molding cycle continues, the worker removes an adequately cooled seat or cover from the cooling bath and performs several finishing operations. He or she drills holes for the rubber bumper pads, and hinges and bevels or rounds off all the rough edges. Some seats go through a buffing and polishing operation to add a high gloss. Finally, the seat and cover are packaged with the necessary hardware and sent to the shipping department.

After removing a seat from the cooling bath, a worker sands all the rough edges against a moving abrasive belt.

Wooden seats

Years ago, toilet seats were made of a solid piece of carved wood covered with white pyroxylin, a form of lacquer. Now, seats are made of a wood composition and painted.

The wooden seat molding department is in a separate section of the plant. In the foreground are the completed seats and covers. In the background are the compression molding machines.

A worker slits the 35-pound bags of wood flour with a knife and dumps them into the mix box, in the background. To avoid inhaling the wood flour, he wears a protective mask.

Hardwoods, usually maple and birch, are purchased in a ground-up form the consistency of baking flour. The wood flour, which comes in 35-pound bags, is dumped into a mix box. Melamine, a plastic resin in powder form, is added to serve as a binder, or cement. It makes up 15 percent of the final volume. A zinc sterate compound is also added to serve as a mold release so that the wood product, once formed in the press, won't stick to the sides of the mold. Once they are mixed, the materials are moved to an attrition mill, which further pulverizes and refines them.

If the model being made is sold in large quantities, the composition is automatically delivered in preweighed portions to a line of loading jigs, or boxes. If the model is only in limited production, the composition is weighed and loaded by hand from scoops. This saves the cost of setting up a complex automated line for a small number of seats. The automatic and manual production lines are in separate sections within the same department.

The operator takes a loaded scoop to one of a series of molding presses and empties it into the bottom half of the mold. Once the composition has been smoothed and evenly distributed, the top half of the mold is lowered. The mold, which only forms a single unit, a seat or a cover, is heated to 300° F. The two halves are held together by 150 tons of pressure for six and a half minutes, during which time the plastic and wood melt together in the thermosetting process.

The hard, woodlike seat or cover is removed from the press, placed on an overhead conveyor system, and moved

In the hand-loading section of the wooden seat molding department are bins containing the wood-melamine mixture. In the foreground, hanging from scales, are scoops filled from these bins. On either side of the bins are the compression molding machines.

The bottom half of the mold on the left holds a precisely measured quantity of wood flour, which will be smoothed out and evenly distributed by hand before the top of the mold is lowered. On the right, the molding machine operator pulls a switch to join the bottom and top halves of the mold under great pressure.

After being dipped in paint, each seat moves on a conveyor system through a vapor chamber.

The seats and covers are brought to the packaging department, where they are inspected, given the proper hardware, and placed in boxes.

The seats and covers have their sharp edges sanded by the abrasive wheel at the left of the worker. In this photograph, only covers are being sanded. After this step, the seats and covers are placed on special holders suspended from an overhead track system.

to a routering station. Here a worker bevels or sands the edges, removing any rough surfaces that may have been formed.

The seat or cover is then placed on a special holding device hanging from a conveyor system and moved to the painting department. The conveyor lowers the seat into a dip tank filled with paint, then raises it and moves it into an enclosed unit called a vapor chamber. A paint solvent is released in a vapor and surrounds the wet unit. This causes any excess paint to flow evenly off the product without leaving any lines or drip marks. The conveyor then moves the seats through a drying oven. This process is repeated three more times, giving each seat two primer and two enamel coats, which produce a finish almost as smooth as plastic.

The painted seat or cover is then moved to the assembly area. Here the properly matched seat, cover, and mounting hardware are assembled, packaged, and readied for shipment. It has taken two and a half hours from molding to packaging, and the seat or cover has traveled over 3 miles on the conveyor system.

BASEBALLS

One of the qualities the major leagues look for in deciding which model of baseball to use is the sound produced when it is hit. The hollow crack of a base hit is the signature of a top-grade ball. This characteristic is determined by the hardball's materials and its method of construction. Size, weight, durability, and liveliness are other variables carefully controlled by the manufacturer. A typical firm will produce twenty-five different models of hardballs as well as several styles of softballs, each model varying in quality and price.

The construction of a baseball begins with the center, or core, which determines both sound and liveliness. There are two kinds of cores, each 1⅜ inches in diameter. One is made by molding a composition of ground-up cork and black rubber. This center is less expensive to make and produces a livelier ball.

The other core is called a cushioned cork center. A small cork sphere the diameter of a nickel is surrounded by a soft black rubber gasket, which in turn is covered by a hard red rubber cover. This core, made by an extrusion, molding, and heat compression process, gives the distinctive sound traditionally associated with major league baseball.

The cores, purchased by the thousands of gross from a special core manufacturer, are delivered to the winding room of the factory. Here each core is covered with three separate layers of wool and polyester yarn and a finish layer of smooth cotton cord. The first layer, or wind, uses four-ply yarn (four thin strands, or plies, twisted into one big strand),

On the left is a composition core, made of cork and black rubber. On the right is a cross section of a cushioned cork center, which consists of a small cork core, a soft black rubber gasket, and a hard red rubber cover. Both cores are 1⅜ inches in diameter.

The cores are brought to the winding room to be wrapped with yarn. The spools of yarn are placed on rotating platforms beneath the winding machine. The worker in the foreground is tying a knot around a core to start the winding operation.

After the yarn is tied to it, the core is placed in a holding fixture. This fixture keeps the ball pressed against a rotating canvas wheel and shakes it from side to side so that the yarn winds onto the ball evenly.

From experience, the machine operator gauges when enough yarn has been wrapped around the core. To check his judgment, the worker places the core in a sizer ring. If there is enough yarn, it will fit snugly.

which is wrapped around the core until the ball measures $2\frac{1}{8}$ inches in diameter. The next wind adds a three-ply yarn, making the ball $3\frac{3}{8}$ inches in diameter. The third wind adds a two-ply yarn, making the ball $3\frac{3}{4}$ inches in diameter. The thin, tight white cotton cord makes up the finish wind, which is only one layer thick and gives the ball its final smooth appearance.

By the fourth wind there are more than two hundred layers of yarn surrounding the core. Finer and finer yarns have been used to give the ball an even surface after the cover is put on. If only a four-ply yarn were used, the surface of the ball would be bumpy because of the spaces between each thick piece of yarn.

The winding is done by four machines, a different one for each thickness of yarn. Each machine winds eight cores at a time. The spools of yarn, located on rotating platforms below the machine, are first threaded through the winder. The rotating platforms help the yarn unwind without twisting. The operator takes a core from a container on top of the machine, ties a knot of yarn around it, and places it in a movable holding fixture pressed against a rotating canvas-covered wheel.

As the core is rotated by the wheel, the holding fixture moves sideways, back and forth, $\frac{1}{2}$ inch in each direction. This is called shaking. Because the rotation of the core is constantly changing, the yarn cannot build up on any section of the core. Instead, an even, spherical coating is wound around it.

The worker can tell when the core has enough yarn wrapped around it by how long it has been on the fixture and how large it is. He removes the wrapped core from the holding fixture, breaks the thread, and passes the core through a testing ring, or sizer, to check its diameter. If it is the proper size, the core is dropped in a box and brought over to the next winding machine.

After the last wind, the balls are taken through a glue-applying setup. A worker, standing on a platform, takes the balls one by one and dips them by hand into a bucket of latex glue. After they absorb the glue for a few seconds, they are rolled down a metal slide to remove the excess adhesive. The balls then fall into a wire basket and are allowed to dry. The outside wind has thus been solidified so that it won't move around when the ball is in play. Now the ball is ready for the outside cover.

The covers for hardballs are made of horsehide or cowhide. The seam, usually sewn together with strong thread, is the most likely part of the ball to fall apart. Horsehide is stronger than cowhide, and tends to retain a stronger seam longer. Better-quality balls are covered with horsehide.

The two-part leather covers are stamped out by an electric press. Five layers of leather are laid out flat on a platform on the press. A cutting steel rule die, shaped like half of the curved cover, is placed over the leather layers. The

The two-part covers are stamped out by an electric press from sheets of leather. A sharp cutting die, held in the worker's right hand, is forced through the leather. The scraps are thrown into a bin, in the foreground, and the covers are packed in a cardboard box.

A worker dips the balls into a pail of white latex glue. To remove the excess glue, the balls are rolled down the metal chute on the right. On the floor, coated balls are drying in wire baskets.

Workers sew on the covers for some softballs by hand.

To label the balls, a worker places them in a holder on a revolving platform. Stamps positioned at different angles in the labeling machine are lowered to print the manufacturer's name and model on each ball.

Each ball is inspected, packed in its own box, and put into a carton to be shipped.

die works like a cookie cutter. One side is as sharp as a razor; the top is a flat section of steel.

After the worker places the die on top of the leather, a hammerlike device is released. The cutting die is forced through the five skins by several tons of pressure. The cut covers are removed and placed in a box. The two sections of the cover are exactly the same and nestle together when fitted around the ball.

Sewing the covers onto the wound ball is time-consuming and takes great skill. Because no machine has been invented to perform this task efficiently, most companies send their product to Haiti to be sewn by hand (labor is much less costly there than in this country). However, some very large models of softballs are hand-sewn in the plant. These are quickly and easily assembled.

When the balls are returned to the manufacturer, they are stamped with the model number and company name. Finally, they are inspected to be sure they meet the standard of quality required before being packed in individual boxes.

BUTTONS

Before World War II buttons were manufactured from many substances. Most buttons were made from seashells but wood, bone, horn, the shells of certain Brazilian nuts, cellulose (a highly flammable plant-derived product), and urea (an animal-derived resin) were commonly used.

Many of the shells from which buttons were cut were gathered by divers off the South Pacific Islands. Button makers bought these shells for ten to fifteen cents a pound. Toward the end of the war, American troops occupied these islands and hired the native divers for many of the unskilled jobs necessary to run a military camp. For this work the islanders were paid wages that were much higher than what they had been receiving for the dangerous work of diving for shells. After realizing the value of their labor, the divers increased the price of shells to almost three dollars a pound.

After the war, plastic technology developed and synthetics began to replace materials traditionally used in making many products. Because of the increased cost of shells, the button industry was an early convert to this popular and inexpensive technology. Today there are 114.2 million gross of plastic buttons made each year, or 81 buttons for each American.

Plastic buttons can be made by several different methods. The injection molding process involves forcing melted plastic into a mold containing many button-shaped cavities. The mold casting method uses plastic slugs, cut from a long rod, which are placed in the bottom half of a two-part mold.

A stainless steel batch kettle, like the one shown at left, holds enough liquid polyester to make all the buttons for a day's run.

The mold is closed and heat and pressure applied to produce a finished button. Die cutting of cylinder-cast polyester sheets, the method used in this factory, is, however, the most common process.

The raw material for die cutting is polyester, a chemical derived from the processing of petroleum. This is delivered by tanker truck every couple of weeks to 36,000-gallon storage tanks built beside the factory. From the storage tanks, the liquid polyester is pumped into stainless steel batch kettles. Each kettle holds enough to provide the raw materials for a day's run. If the buttons being made during a work day are going to be other than the natural translucent color of the polyester, chemical dyes are added. For example, titanium is mixed in if the buttons are to be white; red carbonate, called pearlessence, can be added to give the buttons an artificial shell-like appearance; and carbon black is the dye for black buttons.

The plastic mixture is drawn off from the batch kettles into metal beakers that hold up to three gallons and brought to a mixing table. Here, where the final solution is mixed, a worker adds liquid wax and a catalyst. The catalyst, added in precise proportions, reacts chemically with the polyester and after several minutes makes the polyester harden, or set-up. The wax is added as a releasing agent.

This final mix is taken to the cylinder casting room. Lining the wall of this room are steel cylinders 4 feet in diameter and 2 feet long. The cylinders, which have a smooth, chromed interior, rotate at 250 rpm on their sides on a series of power-driven rollers. A worker slowly pours the mixture from one of the beakers evenly across the inside length of the rotating cylinder. The centrifugal force of the rotation spreads the solution out in an even sheet. A two-inch-high lip around the edges of the cylinder prevents the liquid from running out the ends. The more polyester poured into the cylinder, the thicker the sheet will be. The thickness of the sheet determines the thickness of the button.

A worker carefully pours the final mix of polyester from a small beaker. The rotating cylinder spreads the liquid out in an even sheet from which the buttons will be cut. A two-inch lip around each end of the cylinder prevents the solution from running over.

After the polyester congeals, the worker slits the sheet, carefully peels it off the chromed interior of the cylinder, and rolls it onto the wooden tube to the left of his hand.

As the sheet slowly begins to congeal, the wax rises to the top and bottom surfaces. After rotating for twenty minutes the polyester has hardened to the consistency of a piece of stale cheese. It can easily be crumbled between two fingers. When the casting cycle is over, the cylinder is stopped and a worker slits the sheet and rolls it off onto a wooden tube. Although the releasing wax, which has formed a thin layer between the sheet and the cylinder, makes it easy to peel off, the worker has to be very gentle to prevent it from tearing.

The sheet is taken from the cylinder casting room and laid out on a small conveyer on a blanking machine. As the sheet is advanced by the conveyer, it passes under a series of circular steel rule cutting dies, each die the diameter of a button. These dies are automatically lowered like cookie cutters to punch out small circles of polyester, called blanks, from which the buttons are made. To get as many blanks as possible out of a sheet, and as little waste, the rows are cut very close together. Once cut, the blanks fall down a chute into a basket on the floor.

Blanks of different sizes can be produced simply by changing the cutting dies. There are fifteen different sizes of dies for the fifteen standard-sized buttons manufactured for the

At the top are three steel rule cutting dies. The small, tapered end, which is the diameter of a button, is the edge that cuts the blanks. The other end fits into the die-holding fixture below.

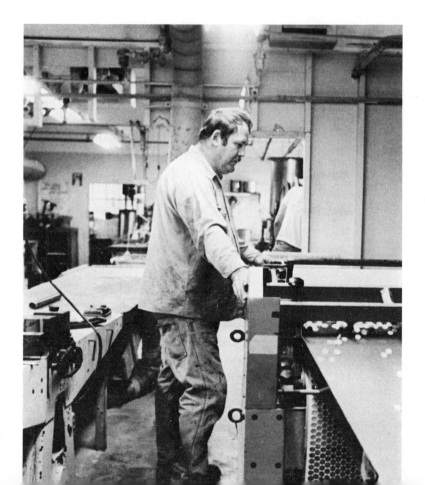

A worker guides a sheet of polyester through the blanking machine. Near his right hand the cutting dies punch out the blanks, which fall down the chute in the foreground into a basket on the floor. The punched-out sheet is visible as it emerges under the chute.

Using a block and tackle, a worker hoists two nylon bags full of hot blanks into the steaming salt water tank. Small, hollow plastic balls that float on the surface help keep the water from cooling below 230° F.

clothing industry in the United States. Depending on the size of the blanks being cut, it takes from two to four minutes to stamp out the 12½-foot-long sheet.

Heat is a byproduct of the reaction between the polyester and the hardening catalyst. This reaction, if not controlled, would cause the blanks to heat up, turn yellow, and start to smoke. To prevent this, the blanks are cooled slowly. If they were cooled too quickly, the plastic would fracture and crack. In order for the blanks to cool properly, they are taken from the baskets beneath the blanking machine and dumped into nylon bags. The bags are then suspended in tanks containing salt water with the same specific gravity as the polyester. The salt water, which is kept at 230° F, keeps the blanks floating inside the bags. Because they are suspended, all the blanks receive equal exposure to the slowly cooling water.

After fifteen minutes in the hot bath, the bags are removed and dipped in a cold water tank to cool them further. The blanks, which are now in their button-hard state, are next dumped into a wire mesh basket in a centrifugal drying machine. As the blanks are spun around at a high speed, all the excess water is thrown off.

Although there are only fifteen different standard sizes, buttons are made in thousands of different styles. A woman's coat manufacturer, for instance, may want a special button with a deep indentation around the holes for a new style coat it is designing. From a profile drawing of the button made by the coat manufacturer, the button company will make a hard carbide-steel cutting tool. The shape of the tool is ground by an abrasive pantograph machine to the exact opposite of the side view of the button. Where there is an indentation in the button, for example, the tool will have a sharp-edged protrusion. The cutting tool is then installed in an indexer or button-making machine.

The blanks, brought in boxes from the drying machine, are dumped into a hopper on top of the index machines. From the hopper they fall into a collet, or holder, and are clamped tight and moved or indexed in front of the cutting tool. The tool, rapidly spinning as it is advanced into the face of the button, cuts the desired shape into it. The cutter is retracted and the button is then indexed in front of a set of drills, which cut the holes. The number of holes, the distance between them, and their diameter are all specified by the clothing manufacturer. After being drilled, the button is vacuumed out of the collet into a box beneath the machines.

On sizes up to a nickel, these button machines can make a gross a minute. Larger buttons, however, and those with a very deep shape cut into them can only be made at a rate of 50 to 70 a minute. A button maker will typically manufacture 700,000 of one type of button a year.

A carbide-steel cutting tool is made in the exact opposite shape of the face of the button. Where there is an indentation in the button, there will be a protrusion in the tool.

A machine operator scoops blanks from the box by his feet and pours them into the hopper at the top of the indexer. This machine cuts the proper shape into the face of the button and drills the holes.

21

The buttons are put into tumbling drums for polishing. The hexagonal shape of the drums causes the buttons to bounce around inside as the drums spin. On the safety gate in front of each drum is a sheet listing the time the buttons were placed in the drum, the type of button, and the required finish.

To remove tool marks, scratches, and sharp edges, the buttons are next dumped into tumbling drums. A fine abrasive pumice, foaming agents, and water are added. As many as 15,000 gross of small shirt buttons at a time are put in these drums and tumbled for up to 24 hours. There are three types of finishes: polished, satin, and dull.

The buttons are washed, removed from the tumbler, dried, and taken to the quality-control department. There they are placed on a small conveyer that passes in front of an inspector. This worker visually checks each button to make sure there are no flaws in its appearance. After being inspected, the buttons are packed in boxes and shipped to the customer.

A quality-control inspector checks each finished button for flaws as it passes before her on a small conveyer belt.

FIRE HYDRANTS

In cities, fire hydrants are placed every 300 feet. Ten feet in front of most hydrants, a small rectangular iron cover is set into the street. This conceals the valve below the street surface that controls the water flow from the water main to the fire hydrant. If a car were to knock over a hydrant, the fire or water department could turn the valve and shut off the water supplying that hydrant while it was being repaired. In areas with old water systems, there is often only one valve for many hydrants, all of which have to be shut off if a single hydrant needs repair.

Most hydrant manufacturers offer a special model, one of several they make, which is designed to collapse when struck by a car. It is made up of many parts so it can be rebuilt easily, without having to replace the whole unit.

Hydrants have from one to three nozzles, depending on their location. In highly populated urban areas there are usually three nozzles, the center one having a larger diameter than the other two. Large hoses are connected to this 5-inch nozzle, and greater amounts of water are permitted to flow to a pumper fire truck. This truck increases the water pressure by pumping and allows the firemen to direct water up to tall buildings.

In areas where the buildings are not as tall, the normal city pressure and smaller nozzles are adequate. The water pressure in most cities ranges from 80 to 90 pounds per square inch (psi). This pressure allows 500 gallons of water a minute to pass through the hydrants.

Old engine blocks, pig iron, and miscellaneous scrap iron are purchased by the hydrant manufacturer from scrap-iron dealers. These and bad castings produced in the factory are the raw materials for fire hydrants.

A fire hydrant has forty parts. Their essential functions revolve around a single component, the check valve. This mechanism is located underground, at the very bottom of the hydrant unit, in a curved bowl-like pipe called the elbow. A long steel rod, the operating stem, protrudes from the top of almost all hydrants and connects to the check valve in the elbow.

To open the hydrant, a fireman takes a special wrench and turns the operating stem, which is usually square or hexagonal. As the stem is turned, it opens the check valve in the elbow. This permits water to flow from the water main up through the hydrant and out the nozzles. This system is designed to prevent water from being in the hydrant until the valve is opened. If water were in the hydrant during the winter, it would freeze, expand, and crack the hydrant.

When a city orders a hydrant, it specifies how far underground the check valve is to be located. In very cold regions the water main and check valve have to be buried from 6 to 8 feet below ground to prevent them from freezing.

Fire hydrants are made in an iron foundry by a casting process. Old automobile engine blocks, which are made from a high-grade cast iron, pig iron, bad castings from the factory, and miscellaneous high-grade scrap cast iron, are the raw materials for hydrants. Cast iron is an alloy made of iron, carbon, and silicon.

These materials are smashed into small pieces with a giant steel ball controlled by a crane. Then the cast iron is loaded into a portable preheater. This unit, which holds 4800 pounds, heats the iron to 850° F. This burns off all the oil, grease, and other nonmetallic substances. The heater is then lifted by a gantry crane and suspended over an electric induction furnace. The bottom of the preheater opens and the iron drops into the furnace. At 2400° F, it takes fifteen to twenty minutes to melt the iron to a molten state.

A hydraulic system tips the furnace and pours the melted iron into a holding ladle. This vessel, shaped like a giant

The tall cylindrical forms at the upper right of the photograph are the preheaters. Once they have burned all the nonmetallic substances out of the cast-iron scrap, they are lifted by a crane and carried over one of the two electric induction furnaces shown at the bottom left. After the cover of the furnace is lifted and the preheater is lowered, the hinged bottom of the preheater is opened, releasing the scrap iron.

A worker wearing a heat-resistant uniform pulls slag, an impurity that forms on the surface of molten iron, out of the furnace. Next, the whole furnace will be hydraulically tipped to fill holding ladles with molten iron.

cup suspended from an overhead track system, is then moved away from the furnace by a worker who walks beside it. The holding ladle is in turn hydraulically tipped over to fill a much smaller pouring ladle. This pouring ladle contains enough molten iron to fill four molds in which four hydrants and their extension pipes are formed.

In brief, the iron is poured, or cast, into a mold that permits the liquid iron to flow into the hollow form of a hydrant. The mold is devised by making an impression of the front half of a hydrant in a sand and coal mixture contained in a metal frame. Placed inside this impression is a hardened sand core shaped almost exactly like the fire hydrant except that is $\frac{3}{8}$ inch smaller in every dimension. A frame with an impression of the back half of the hydrant, also in a sand and coal mixture, is then placed over the two units. The molten iron is poured into the $\frac{3}{8}$-inch channel formed between the suspended core within the hydrant-shaped impressions. The sand is removed, leaving the hollow hydrant.

In more detail, to begin with, several operations are necessary to make the mold. Two separate sections of hardwood are machined and turned on a lathe to the outside dimensions of half of the hydrant. The front section is called

The wooden master pattern is laid out on a pattern holder so it can be worked on easily.

the cope; the back is the drag. Rounded sections are also machined for the lower extension pipes. Together these forms are called the master pattern.

Instead of having a hollow opening for the nozzles, the master pattern is constructed with solid wood protrusions extending several inches from where the nozzle opening will be in the hydrant. These are called the core prints and are crucial to the casting of the hollow hydrant.

Once they are finished, the masters are brought to another section of the plant and pressed into a mixture of compressed sand and coal contained in a metal frame called a flask. When the master pattern is removed from the flask, an impression is left in the sand and coal mixture: one impression for the front half of the hydrant and extension pipe and one for the back section. Melted plastic or aluminum is poured into these impressions and allowed to cool and harden before it is removed. These plastic or aluminum castings are called the permanent patterns.

Two permanent patterns of copes (fronts) are placed in a holder face up in a machine called a big Herman. A flask is lowered around them. Sand high in clay content and pulverized coal dust is emptied by a conveyor feed system into the flask, covering the patterns. The coal dust is added to help prevent the sand from sticking to the molten iron as it cools. The big Herman vibrates and compresses, with several tons' pressure, the sand and coal mixture on top of the patterns.

The flask is then lifted off the patterns, removed from the Herman, and turned over. The sand and coal mixture is

The master pattern is used to cast an aluminum or plastic permanent pattern, seen in this photograph. Upside down on the right is the front of the hydrant, called the cope. On the left is the back, or the drag. Extending from the nozzle openings (for the water hoses) are solid protrusions called core prints. These are essential in casting the hollow hydrant.

The aluminum pattern for the hydrant and its extension pipes have been placed in the lower section of this machine, called a big Herman. The worker at the control panel is directing a flask to be lowered around the permanent pattern.

27

This flask contains the sand and coal mixture in which two impressions of the drag have been made. Note the core prints extending out of the nozzles.

compressed so firmly in the flask that none of it falls out. Pressed into its surface is the impression of the two copes. This process is repeated for the drags (backs). In addition to the exact shape of the outside of the hydrant, the impression contains the core prints, which appear in the flasks as indentations protruding out of the nozzles.

To form the inside of the hydrant, a two-part wooden core box is constructed. Inside each half of the rectangular box, the configuration of half of the inside of the hydrant is carved out. Sand with a glue binder is mixed and rammed into the hollow cavity formed when the two halves are joined. Carbon dioxide is forced through the mixture to draw off all the moisture in the sand.

The core box is then separated and the solid core of sand removed. The core is shaped like the fire hydrant, except that it is $\frac{3}{8}$ inch smaller in every dimension. Like the mas-

ter and permanent patterns, the core has the solid protrusion of several inches where the nozzles are.

The cope and drag flasks are moved from the big Herman to the casting room. A core is placed in each impression in the cope flask. The solid protrusions out of the nozzles in the core rest upon the core prints made in the sand and coal by the permanent pattern. Resting upon the core prints, the core is suspended ⅜ inch from the impression in the cope flask. The drag flask is then lifted and placed directly over the top half of the core. The two flasks are then bolted together. The completed mold, with the ⅜-inch channel created between the core and impressions in the cope and drag flasks, is ready to receive the molten iron.

A worker, wearing a special heat-resistant uniform, pours 450 pounds of iron from the pouring ladle into a channel hole on top of the mold. As the iron fills the ⅜-inch channel, great clouds of steam and vapor escape. The steam is produced by the reaction of the molten iron with the moisture in the sand of the cope and drag flasks. Because the sand has a higher melting point than the molten iron, the sand in the cores, copes, and drags is essentially unaffected. Coal, which is used to help prevent the sand from fusing to the surface of the molten-iron casting, burns up in the heat of this reaction.

The iron, contained in the ⅜-inch channel between the core and flasks, assumes the hollow shape of the fire hydrant. The core forms the hollow inside of the hydrant, and the impressions in the flasks shape the outside surfaces.

Cores made of hard sand have been placed in the impressions in the drag flask. Extending from the nozzles are the core prints, which fit into those in the previous photograph. When these protrusions rest in the core prints, they hold the core ⅜ inch above the impression of the hydrant in the flask, creating the space into which the molten iron will flow.

The cope flask and the drag flask are clamped together, with the core suspended in the center of the two impressions.

29

A worker controls the pouring ladle, which is suspended from an electrically powered hoist system. The ladle is tipped to pour the molten iron into the channel hole in the mold.

The castings are allowed to cool, and the two flasks are separated and placed on a vibrating screen to shake the sand out of the flasks. The sand falls onto a conveyor belt, to be returned to the mulling room to be remixed with coal and used again in the big Herman. The hydrants, which still have the sand cores inside them, are lifted by chains and put into holders in a machine called a wheelabrator. The wheelabrator is a large chamber with a rotating circular platform.

Workers remove the special valve castings for municipal water systems from the wheelabrator. Next, they will load the cooled hydrant castings in the foreground onto the round platform. The platform swings into the wheelabrator at left and the door behind the platform closes.

Because small amounts of iron escaped between the two halves of the mold during the casting, the hydrant has sharp, rough seams. These are called flashings. Steel balls, ½ inch in diameter, called shot, are placed in the wheelabrator, the door is closed, and the platform with the hydrant castings in their holders is rapidly rotated. The shot bounces around inside the chamber, knocks off the flashings, and causes the sand core to collapse and fall out of the hydrant. The platform is stopped, and the hydrants are removed from the chamber and brought to the finishing area. Using power hand tools, workers grind down any remaining rough surfaces.

The hydrants are then moved to the machine shop, where threads are cut into the nozzles so caps, and later fire hoses, can be screwed on. Holes are drilled to allow the hydrants and extension pipes to be bolted together. The hydrants are then moved to a small assembly line. Here they are joined with the check valves, stems, covers, caps, chains, gaskets, bushings, couplings, nuts, and other hardware that make up the completed hydrant. Finally, the hydrants are painted with a rust-resistant paint, allowed to dry, and moved outdoors to a holding area in preparation for shipping.

Fire hydrants cost between $300 and $350 apiece. The fire departments in most cities and towns take good care of this

In the assembly area, the central castings are joined with the valves, stems, caps, couplings, and assorted hardware to complete the hydrant.

The finished hydrants lie outdoors to await shipping to towns and cities. The rounded form at the bottom of the extension pipes is the elbow that contains the check valve.

municipal investment. Twice a year, usually in the spring and fall, the hydrants are opened and flushed. This clears out any stagnant water, mineral deposits, and rocks or pebbles collected in the hydrant or main. These foreign materials could damage and impair the use of the hydrant. Such preventive maintenance guarantees a long and useful life for these devices.

Nevertheless, each year thousands of hydrants are destroyed by automobiles. In addition, in the winter, water sometimes passes through faulty check valves into the hydrants and freezes, cracking either the extension pipes or the hydrants themselves. These factors support an industry that produces tens of millions of dollars' worth of new hydrants a year, with a single company producing more than 8000 hydrants a month.

PAINT BRUSHES

You get what you pay for when you buy a paintbrush. A typical manufacturer makes fifty different styles and models of brushes. The quality and quantity of the materials and the workmanship are carefully controlled to produce brushes that vary from the throwaway product, made to be used once or twice and then discarded, to those made to last professional painters a lifetime.

Before the advent of synthetics, all paintbrushes were made from natural bristles shaved primarily from hogs. The best brushes were made from bristles imported from China. These bristles were used when there was only one kind of paint available, oil-based. Bristle brushes are still made with materials imported from Poland, southern Europe, and South America.

About the same time that water-based latex paint was developed, synthetic fiber bristles were invented. The first ones were nylon. Brushes made of nylon bristles had two advantages over those made of natural bristles: they were less expensive and could be used with either water- or oil-based paint (natural bristles tend to soften because of the water in latex paint). However, synthetic brushes were easily affected by heat. Often, when the brushes were on display in store windows, the sun's heat, magnified by the glass, would cause the fibers to sag and melt. Today, most of the brushes manufactured are made from synthetic fiber bristle. One synthetic fiber commonly used is the petroleum-derived polyester.

A paintbrush is made up of fibers, a ferrule, a cardboard plug, and a handle.

When buying a brush, a professional painter will squeeze it to see how much body it has, flex it to feel its stiffness and recovery qualities, and heft it to feel its weight. Like a baseball player and his favorite bat, a painter has his or her own feelings about what makes a good brush. Some judge by weight, others by the brush's flexibility.

The most important factor in a good brush is the amount of bristle that it contains. Essentially, it is the bristle that determines how well a brush works, and the brush manufacturer varies the amount used as well as its taper, length, and the shape of the ends to produce many different qualities in a brush.

All brushes have a stiff cardboard plug that is inserted in the base in the middle of the bristles. When you separate the bristles, you can see the top part of the plug. This plug creates a well, or reservoir, that allows the brush to hold more paint when it is dipped than the bristles could alone. The paint gently flows out of the reservoir and down the bristles to the tip of the brush. An inexpensive brush, with a large plug and less bristle, will have a tendency to drip, and the paint will not flow evenly.

Taper ratio also determines the quality of a brush. This term describes the difference in thickness, or diameter, between the two ends of each bristle. The bristle at the tip of the brush is smaller than the end near the handle, called the butt. For example, a thin bristle might be 6/1000 inch at the tip and 9/1000 at the butt. A thick bristle, which would make for a stiffer brush, would be 10/1000 at the tip and 18/1000 at the base. Taper helps the paint flow toward the tip of the bristle and allows the brush to be firm yet flexible. The most inexpensive brushes have single-diameter bristles, with no taper. Synthetic fiber bristles imitate the natural taper of hog bristles.

All brushes made of synthetic fibers, whether tapered or not, have the first ½ inch of the fibers split, or flagged. This is normally the only portion of the brush that touches the surface to be painted. A fiber bristle, which may, for example, be 6/1000 inch in diameter at its tip, is split at least three or four times. This increases the number of fiber ends that apply the paint. When you hold a single bristle up to a light, you can easily see the finely split tips.

A synthetic bristle is an extruded filament made from chemicals derived from either coal or petroleum. The bristle is purchased from large chemical companies in lengths ranging from 1 to 4½ inches. A brush of any size can have from one to five different lengths of fiber. The variation in lengths causes the flagged ends of the bristle, the part that applies the paint most effectively, to cluster at the last ½ inch of the brush. This formation promotes an even and smooth application of the paint. The better the brush, the more different lengths it has. A brush made with a single length of fiber has a tendency to streak, and only the very tip can be used to apply the paint.

Fiber bristles come in different lengths and taper ratios. The bundles here show two different lengths and two possible taper ratios within each length.

There is a simple way to test a brush to find out how many different lengths it contains. Hold the brush in one hand and lay a finger of your other hand across the butt perpendicular to the brush. Bending the fibers down, slowly move your finger toward the tip. As your finger moves along, different lengths of fiber bristles, evenly mixed throughout the brush, will pop up.

Cardboard boxes filled with small bundles of fiber of the same length and taper ratio are received by the brushmaker. First, the bristles are prepared for the flagging and tipping operations. A clump of fibers is inserted into a chuck, or holder, with the tapered end up. Air is injected into the chuck to inflate the rubber diaphragm that surrounds and firmly holds the base of the fibers in place.

The chucks are then clamped on top of a spinning fixture, which slowly revolves under a set of flagging blades turning at 5000 rpm. The razor-sharp blades split ⅓ inch of the top of each fiber into several strands.

Once the ends are split, the fibers pass under a set of five rotating stone grinding wheels. These abrasive wheels act like a pencil sharpener on the spinning fibers, grinding a sharp point on each of the split strands. This operation is

Bundles of fibers are placed in round chucks with inflatable rubber diaphragms, which hold the bristles tightly in place.

Round, razor-sharp flagging blades are connected in a series on a central core.

called tipping. The grinding wheels are lubricated with water to prevent the heat caused by friction from melting the bristles. After being tipped, the bristles are removed from the chucks, banded together, and repacked in boxes.

A fiber bristle mixture is then prepared according to the specific formula for the size and quality of the brush being made. Bristles of the proper lengths and taper ratios are laid out on a mixing machine. A formula may call for five different lengths in three taper ratios, which are laid out, one size on top of another. The mixture, which weighs from 8 to 10 pounds, is folded into itself more than ten times, until no single clump of any given size can be found.

The mixed bristles are then brought to the brushmaking machines and placed in a hopper, or pocket. A small fork-like device called a picker is adjusted to pull from the hopper, according to weight, the right amount of bristles for the brush being made. Thin, or flagged, ends first, the fibers are pushed into the ferrule, the metal band surrounding the bristles on all paintbrushes. The ferrules, stamped out of thin tin-coated steel, are purchased from another manufacturer.

The ferrules containing the fibers are automatically placed on a moving conveyor system. A series of patting devices, like small metal hands, gently pat the fibers into the ferrule. When the fibers are about halfway through the ferrule, the brush enters the plugging station, where a tapered, hollow knife advances into middle of the butt ends of the fibers and separates them. A flat piece of stiff cardboard, cut to the right size from a large roll, is inserted through the hollow knife and into the brush until it is flush with the butts of

The proper assortment of fiber lengths and taper ratios for one model of brush is laid out on the table in the foreground. The worker places a specific amount of each type of fiber, weighed on the scale at the left, into the folding machine. After the fibers have been thoroughly mixed and combined, the completed batches are laid out on the table in the background.

In the upper left section of the photograph, the last of a series of metal hands pats the bristles into the ferrules. Only the tips of the bristles are visible in a line; the rest and the ferrules are hidden by the machine. The worker removes the bristles that haven't been properly pushed into the ferrules.

The worker injects glue from the dispenser onto the butt ends of the fibers recessed in the ferrules.

the fibers. The fibers and plug are patted several more times until they are even with the top edge of the ferrule. A gripper then grabs the flagged ends of the brush and pulls the bristles until they are ¼ inch from the top of the ferrule.

The brushes are removed from the conveyor belt and gently placed, tips down, in wooden boxes and brought to the glue machine. A two-part glue (one part epoxy resin, the other a catalyst and curing agent) is prepared in tanks in the machine. Because the epoxy dries so quickly once it is mixed, the two parts are kept apart until minutes before they are used. A worker presses a trigger on the dispensing device, which activates a metered pump. The pump

In this finishing machine, a series of blades cuts the bristles into the proper shape. The machine also aligns, combs, and cleans the bristles.

These brushes have been placed in wooden boxes to be taken to the assembly machine, where they will be joined to their handles.

forces out a precise amount of glue onto the butts of the fibers contained in the ferrule, one brush at a time. The glue is designed to penetrate ½ inch through the butt.

After several hours of drying in a ventilated chamber, the brushes are taken to the finishing machine, which performs two functions. It cuts and shapes the fiber bristles into different configurations, depending on the brush's intended use: an angular shape for painting window sashes, an oval form for trim and pipes, or a high-quality chiseled model for flat painting. Then the machine reflags and tips the bristles that have been partially cut off in shaping and aligns, combs, and cleans all the bristles.

Now the brushes are ready to be joined with the handles. If the brush is a high-production, inexpensive model, it is brought to an automated assembly machine. Plastic handles manufactured by a custom injection molding company are used because they are less expensive and tend to stand up to abuse longer than wooden ones. The brushes and handles are piled into separate feeding ramps, and the two parts are automatically joined. The handle is fitted snugly into the ferrule, flush against the glued bristles. Four rivets are forced through the metal ferrule and fastened into the handle. Expensive brushes, made for professional painters who know how to clean and maintain them, are hand-fitted with wooden handles manufactured by a wood-shaping company.

The worker piles the brushes into a vertical feeding ramp on the assembly machine. Below his arm, another vertical ramp contains the handles. The assembled brushes leave from the far side of the machine, not shown.

The best-selling brushes made are the 1½-inch, tapered, single-length models. They are inexpensive because they can be produced by machines at a rate of forty a minute. These brushes are generally made for the nonprofessional, who will use the brush once or twice. Brush manufacturers describe the use of this brush as the smear method of applying paint. Basically, the brush serves as a vehicle to get the paint from the can to the painting surface, where it is rather unevenly pushed around.

The spectrum of quality and workmanship in making a brush is so broad that a medium-sized company can provide a mass-produced consumer item while retaining the ability to fashion a well-made, hand-crafted product.

MATCHES

When matches first became popular in the 1830s, they were known as lucifers. With approximately 500 billion matches made and consumed each year in the United States, five times the numbers of stars in our galaxy, the devil is well remembered.

These portable sources of fire are manufactured in factories so safe that insurance companies would rather insure them than private homes. A typical match company is a safety-conscious, highly automated plant, which produces millions of matchbooks a day.

Most match manufacturers are in the giveaway end of the industry. An advertiser, a correspondence school, for example, will pay to have its message printed on 50 million books of matches. The manufacturer produces the matches and sells them to a vendor, perhaps a company that distributes cigarettes to supermarkets, at about $7 a case. Contrary to the practice in other countries, the matches are usually given away to the final consumer.

The production of book matches is a three-part operation: the fabrication of the matches, the preparation of the cover, and the assembly of the two parts.

Thousand-pound rolls of recycled paperboard a little more than a foot wide are received from several different paper mills. (A single paper mill usually can't supply the paper demands of one match company.) The paperboard, which has a dark side and a light side, has been treated at the mill with a chemical fire retardant, diammonium phosphate.

In the foreground are the 13-inch-wide rolls of recycled paperboard from which the lights are made. The 39-inch-wide rolls of cover stock can be seen in the background.

This chemical helps slow down the burning of the match and prevents afterglow as the match burns out.

The rolls are moved to die-cutting, or blanking, machines. These machines cut the stock into 1¾-inch strips, called splints, at a rate of several hundred a minute. Each splint has a solid, uncut base ⅜ inch wide with one hundred and twenty sections cut above it. Each section will be an individual match, or light. Every other light on each splint is bent down at a slight angle during the cutting operation. This allows for adequate space between the matches when the chemicals that make up the head are later applied. Occasionally the heads of two matches are fused together because not enough space separated them.

Once they have been cut on the blanking machines, the splints are forced onto a moving belt that has small metal

The roll of paperboard in the foreground is being cut into strips, called splints, by the blanking machine in the rear.

spikes protruding from its surface. These spikes firmly hold the base of the splints perpendicular to the belt throughout the matchmaking process.

After the splints have been inserted, the belt curls over so the splints hang downward. The splints are then moved to a vat of melted paraffin. Paraffin is a petroleum wax and appears as the darkened part of the match under the head. It prolongs the strong flame after the matchhead has burned out. Seven-sixteenths inch of the hanging splints pass through the bath of paraffin. To keep the paraffin from hardening too quickly, which would prevent the wax from effectively soaking into the paperboard splints, the conveyor belt moves them through a hot oven for half a minute. The paraffin is allowed to harden as the splints move on toward a second vat, called the head bath.

The major ingredient that causes a match to burn is potassium chlorate. Sulfur and potassium bichromate are used in much smaller proportions as additional firing agents.

As the splints leave the blanking machine, they are forced onto a moving belt with protruding spikes, which firmly holds them upside down. In the foreground is a sample splint.

44

The matchhead solution is mixed in this room. At left are the mixing drums; at right, some of the ingredients and a scale for measuring them.

Ground glass, silica, and diatomacious earth (the fossil remains of sea algae) are used both to control the rate of burn and to make the head the proper size. An animal-derived glue and a vegetable starch are the bonding agents that hold the ingredients together. These materials are weighed precisely and mixed according to a definite formula.

Looking closely at a matchhead under a light, one can see the small shiny particles of ground glass. Some match firms add a chemical dye, red or blue, to the yellowish white solution. These colors have no effect on how the match burns. Each manufacturer uses a slightly different formula, mostly for economic reasons, in its head solution. Just below the striker on the cover of all matches is the name of the manufacturer. Matches lit from books made by different companies often burn with different speeds and colors.

For safety, the chemical solution for the matchhead is mixed in a special room in the basement of the plant. It is then pumped up to form the head bath, through which the splints pass after leaving the oven. This bath has rotating rollers that push the solution onto the tips of the splints as they pass through. The speed of both the conveyor belt and the rollers is controlled so that just the right amount of solution is applied to the front and back of each light.

After the head has been applied to the splints, they are moved up to the second level of the plant, to the drying room. For thirty minutes the conveyor belt moves the matches

In the drying room, the coated matches pass over seven tiers on the conveyor belt for thirty minutes, as warm air is gently circulated around them.

back and forth over seven tiers while warm air is gently circulated about the room. It is essential that the matches dry slowly from the inside out. If the head dries too quickly at too high a temperature, the outside dries faster and becomes much harder than the interior. Such a match would produce a small explosion, or pop, when struck.

Humidity is also an important factor in the drying process; the more moisture in the air, the longer the drying time. On rainy days the belt is slowed down to allow more drying time; it is speeded up during dry periods. Some match factories, particularly in the South, have to dehumidify the drying room because of the high moisture level.

The dried splints, still on the spiked conveyor belt, are moving to another level of the factory to be joined with the cover.

Rolls of cover stock, with the striker strip applied, are in the foreground. The center machine is a web press, which prints the covers.

After the splints are dried, the conveyor belt moves them to the assembly area to be joined to the matchbook covers, which have been prepared in another section of the plant.

The cover stock is purchased in rolls the width of three opened matchbooks laid end to end. Each roll weighs more than a half a ton. The rolls of cover stock are taken to the cover machine, which performs three operations. First, it applies the striker strip. Since book matches are safety matches, they can only be lit by the chemical reaction between the matchhead and the striker strip. The striker strip, $\frac{1}{4}$ inch wide, is made of red phosphorus combined with glue (for adherence to the cover). It is the chemical reaction between the red phosphorus on the strip and the potassium chlorate in the matchhead that ignites the match. The two chemicals are kept as far apart as possible in the factory.

The striker-strip applicator on the cover machine has three sponge-covered rotating wheels a booklength apart. The wheels are half-submerged in the striker solution all the time. Three strips are applied as the cover stock passes over the saturated sponge wheels. The coated stock then passes into a heating chamber to dry, after which it passes back to the cover machine for the second and third procedures.

During the second step, a high-speed printing machine, called a web press, prints the customer's advertising in several colors on both sides of the cover. As the cover stock

After the splints have been automatically removed from the spiked conveyor belt, they fall onto a second conveyor belt, which passes through the assembly area.

nears the end of the press, it passes through two cutting blades. This third operation slits and winds the stock into three separate rolls, each the width of a single opened matchbook cover.

The rolls of covers are then brought to the assembly area, where there are several stations on a highly automated line. The match splints, which have come from the drying room, are mechanically removed from the spiked conveyor belt and laid flat on a second conveyor system. A worker at each of the assembly stations takes a handful of splints from the passing conveyor belt and feeds them into an assembling machine.

The assembling machine, which makes hundreds of books a minute, feeds two splints at a time and cuts a ten-match section from each. The cover stock, which rests on a rotating wheel next to the assembler, is automatically cut to the proper length in the machine and folded a little below the striker strip. The two ten-match sections, one on top of the other, are placed in the fold in the cover. A staple is then fastened through the cover and the base of the two splints, and the cover is automatically folded over the splints and closed.

Because of the staggered die-cutting of the splints, the finished matchbooks appear to have four rows of five matches each. It has taken less than an hour from die-cutting to assembling.

After being stapled and closed, the matchbooks are fed onto a small conveyor belt, and every other matchbook is automatically turned upside down for efficient packing into small boxes called caddies. The filled caddies, containing fifty books each, are moved to the packaging department. There they are wrapped with a printed paper cover and packed into cartons, fifty to a box. The cartons are loaded into trailer trucks that distribute them to cigarette vendors and supermarket suppliers.

A worker places the splints, two at a time, on the assembly machine.

In the foreground, splints enter the assembler two at a time. Completed matchbooks can be seen emerging to the right of the roll of staple wire. Every other book is turned upside down for efficient packing.

An employee in the quality-control department continuously samples matches taken from the production line to make sure they meet specifications.

RUBBER BANDS

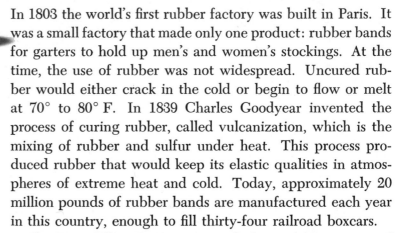

In 1803 the world's first rubber factory was built in Paris. It was a small factory that made only one product: rubber bands for garters to hold up men's and women's stockings. At the time, the use of rubber was not widespread. Uncured rubber would either crack in the cold or begin to flow or melt at 70° to 80° F. In 1839 Charles Goodyear invented the process of curing rubber, called vulcanization, which is the mixing of rubber and sulfur under heat. This process produced rubber that would keep its elastic qualities in atmospheres of extreme heat and cold. Today, approximately 20 million pounds of rubber bands are manufactured each year in this country, enough to fill thirty-four railroad boxcars.

The Post Office Department, which uses 10 percent of this output, has very precise specifications for this product. There are three characteristics used to describe rubber bands: elasticity, tensile strength, and permanent set. Most specifications call for 700 percent elongation; that is, a 1-inch band should be elastic enough to stretch out to 7 inches before breaking. Tensile strength describes the number of pounds of pull it takes to break a band, measured in pounds per square inch. The permanent set is the measurement of how well the rubber band returns to its original shape and size after being stretched. The government standard for this recovery is to within 5 percent of its original size.

The Post Office buys high-quality bands because they constantly reuse them. Newspaper delivery services, on the other hand, buy very inexpensive bands that are designed to be used only once, in wrapping the paper for doorstep

Boxes filled with the more than fifteen ingredients that make rubber bands are placed on a roller system. The materials are dumped in the proper order into a banbury mixer, the top of which can be seen below the boxes in the center of the photograph.

delivery. Predictably, the quality of a rubber band is determined by the materials used in making it. The raw materials for rubber bands can be either synthetic or natural. Both types look alike and have the same general qualities and characteristics. The costs of these raw materials are about the same, but each varies according to world supply and demand. The rubber band manufacturer generally uses whichever material is currently less expensive.

Since rubber bands are purchased, usually in bulk, by the pound, the cost of the materials is important. A manufacturer can produce cheaper bands by using less natural or synthetic rubber and more fillers or extenders, such as clay or reprocessed rubber. Two identical bands, one with extenders, the other without, will perform differently. The band with the fillers will be less elastic. In order to meet the 700 percent elongation requirement, they must have a thicker wall to keep them from breaking when they are stretched. Because the wall is thicker and the band heavier, the number of bands per pound will be fewer. Many manufacturers guarantee the count, or number, of bands in a pound. This is an assurance of both quality and quantity.

The modern formulas for both natural and synthetic rubber consist of more than fifteen different ingredients and chemical compounds, which are precisely measured and mixed before they are vulcanized. The materials have to be added in a special order so that they will react with each other in a predictable way.

Styrene, which is derived from coal, and butadiene, a petroleum product, are the basic ingredients of synthetic rubber. Natural rubber is obtained from the sap of the rubber tree. Zinc oxide, carbon black, sulfur or other curing agents, and accelerators, to speed the chemical bonding of the compounds, are used in both synthetic and natural rubber.

At the start of the manufacturing process, the materials are placed in boxes with a capacity of 30 pounds and moved to a two-story blending machine called a banbury. A worker dumps enough of the ingredients into the mixer to make a 400-pound batch. The banbury churns and heats the materials to 250° F for ten to twelve minutes.

When the banbury cycle is finished, the doughlike mixture is dumped one floor below, directly into a rubber mill. This is a machine with two parallel 7-foot steel rollers that turn against each other like an old-fashioned, hand-cranked washing machine wringer.

After the materials have been heated and blended by the banbury, they are released and fall between the two counter-rotating steel cylinders of the rubber mill.

The rubber falls between the two rollers, which are moving against each other at different speeds. This causes the mixture to be kneaded and folded over many times to produce a smooth and even consistency. As the cylinders rotate, a sheet of rubber is formed on the front cylinder that is ½ inch thick, the distance between the two rollers.

As the sheet forms, two revolving knives pressed against the cylinders cut it into 8-inch strips. These continuous strips are automatically pulled off the cylinder, piled into a large basket on wheels, cut free, and rolled to the extruding machine. Before being piled into a hopper, the strips are coated with a layer of powdered talc, which acts as a lubricant in the extruding process. The rubber is fed from the hopper into the extruding machine, which, like a hand-cranked meat grinder, forces the rubber out an extruding head.

The extruding head uses an annular die. This consists of a ring of steel with a separate, smaller solid core centered inside it. Narrow arms attached to the outer ring hold the core in place. The die works like the nozzle for a garden hose. When the nozzle is adjusted to spray, the water flows around the central pin, or core, in the middle of the nozzle opening. In a similar way, the extruding machine forces the rubber through the space between the ring and the core.

The doughlike rubber is kneaded by the rotating cylinder and forced into a sheet on the front cylinder. A pair of rotating blades, pressed against the front cylinder, moves slowly from side to side, cutting a continuous strip of rubber 8 inches wide. The strip is automatically pulled off the cylinder, as can be seen on the left side of the photograph. The two rotating blades are just visible at the base of the strip.

The strip of rubber is pulled from the canvas basket behind the worker and fed into the top of the extruder. The rubber is forced through the dies and comes out as a hollow tube at the bottom left. This particular tube is a narrow one, for making small rubber bands. A photograph could not be taken of the modern high-speed extruder because it is a new model designed by this rubber band company. This is an older extruding machine.

Two inflated rubber tubes, at the right, enter the 100-foot-long vulcanizing bath. The molten salt is in the bottom half of the vulcanizing structure. The top half helps contain the heat. Two sections on the side are open so that the tubes can be inspected.

Because of the great pressure, the rubber flows around the arms that hold the core in place and comes together again to form a solid tube as it is extruded. The thickness of the wall of the rubber band is determined by the distance between the ring and the core. The diameter of the annular die defines the length of the rubber band: the larger the diameter, the longer the rubber band.

Inside the center of the solid core of the die is an opening for the release of compressed air. As the continuous hollow tube of rubber is extruded through the die, air is pumped into it to keep the tube open. This tube is then pulled through a 100-foot-long tank, or bath, of liquefied salt, which is kept at 370° F. The salt solution is the modern method of vulcanizing both natural and synthetic rubber compounds. The tube is pulled through the bath at a speed that allows the rubber to remain in the salt for no more than a minute.

As the tube leaves the bath, it passes beneath a heavy steel roller, which acts as a seal to keep the air in the tube while it is in the bath and at the same time compresses and creases the tube. This crease gives the rubber band its flattened, elliptical shape.

The tube is then pulled through a solvent washing bath to remove the talc and is moved to the cutting machine. As it

After the tubes exit (at right) from the vulcanizing bath, they pass under a set of rollers. These act as a seal both to keep the air in the tubes behind them and to flatten out the tubes in front, giving them their final, oblong shape.

This vulcanized tube has been flattened into the final shape of the rubber band.

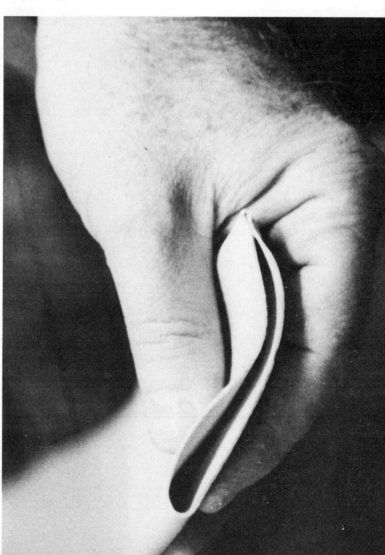

The vulcanized tubes pass through a liquid solvent drum, on the left, to remove the lubricating talc. The tubes then automatically move to the right, to a whirling cutting blade. After being cut, the bands are sucked up through vacuum pipes and can be seen dropping into the canvas basket in front of the worker.

is fed under a circular knife, the tube is cut into bands of rubber. The combination of the speed of the knife and the speed of the tube passing under it determines how wide the bands will be. The slower the speed, the wider the bands; faster speeds produce narrower widths.

A system of vacuum pipes suck up the cut bands, by the billions, and deposit them into canvas baskets. They are labeled by size and delivered to the packing room. There the bands are hand-packed into boxes, checked for proper weight, sealed, and prepared for shipping.

In the metal basket is the continuous rubber tube before it has been cut into rubber bands. In the background are canvas baskets containing the cut bands.

NAILS

Most of the nails used in the United States are imported from Japan. Of the more than 297,000 tons of nails manufactured in this country, the vast majority are produced by the major steel companies. The steel producers make a limited number of sizes and styles of nails, usually called common nails. These are used for a variety of purposes, for example, in new home construction. They are generally sold by the pound in hardware stores.

Nails for special applications made of metals other than carbon steel are produced by smaller, independent nail manufacturers. These firms purchase their raw materials, coils of wire rod, from steel producers or from companies that make stainless steel, copper, and aluminum. These smaller firms have the flexibility to produce limited quantities of many different types of nails. In the same day, for example, a company can make both a short, blunt-pointed nail ordered by a children's crib manufacturer and a stainless steel nail for fabricating wooden boxes for growing mushrooms. The stainless steel nail will never rust and contaminate the growing mushrooms.

The diameter of wire rod is 7/32 inch, about the thickness of a pencil. Each coil weighs, on the average, about 3000 pounds. The coils are brought from a central warehouse to the drawing room. In this part of the factory are several wire drawing machines, which stretch or draw the wire rod, decreasing its initial size to the diameter of the nail desired. For instance, by pulling the wire through a series of progressively smaller drawing dies, the rod can be reduced from

These are coils of wire from which nails are made.

This is a seven-block drawing machine. The original coil of wire is placed at the far end of the machine and drawn through the small round drawing blocks. After each block, the wire wraps around a tall take-up spindle before proceeding left to the next block.

its original size of 7/32 inch to 1/32 inch. This size nail might be used to fasten the corners of large picture frames together.

First, the coil of wire rod is placed on a rotating holder next to the drawing machine. The end of the wire is pulled off the coil, sharpened — or pointed — like a pencil in a pencil sharpener, and inserted into a hole in a circular drawing die. The die is bolted into a boxlike holding fixture called a block that applies a soaplike lubricant to the wire rod. The wire, which is thicker than the hole in the die, can fit through because the first several inches have been pointed.

The drawing machine has seven blocks, each containing a hardened steel die with a tapered hole in the middle. The diameter of the front of the hole is larger than the diameter in the back, and the die is tapered so that, as the wire is pulled through the smaller hole, it is gradually thinned and lengthened without its breaking.

Once the end of the wire is put through the die, it is clamped onto a chain connected to a rotating take-up spindle on top of the drawing machine. When the spindle is started, the wire is pulled through the first die. Depending

Inside each drawing block is a die like this one. The diameter of the front of the hole is larger than the diameter of the back. As the wire is pulled through, it is gradually made longer and thinner.

on the size of the nail desired, each of the seven drawing dies can reduce the diameter of the wire from 17 to 25 percent. If 1000 feet of wire passes through a die with a 17 percent reduction, the wire will be lengthened to 1170 feet as well as thinned.

After several loops have been wrapped around the first spindle, the end of the wire rod is again pointed, threaded through the second die, and clamped onto the second spindle. This further reduces the diameter of the wire. This procedure can be repeated up to seven times, depending on how much the rod is to be reduced. Larger nails, which are closer to the original diameter of the wire rod, need be drawn through only one or two dies.

After the wire has been threaded through the last die and around the last spindle, the drawing machine is started with

The wire travels from the take-up spindle, on the right, through the drawing block, at the left. A drawing die like the one in the previous photograph is bolted inside the block.

all the spindles turning at once. Because the wire is longer after going through each die, every take-up spindle must be adjusted to rotate faster than the previous one to draw and take up the thinner and longer wire. For some wire diameters, the last spindle must rotate nine times faster than the first one. After about 200 pounds of wire have accumulated on the last spindle, the wire is cut, removed from the machine, and brought to the cutting room.

Lined up along the length of this room are more than eighty nail-cutting machines, which cut and form the wire rod into nails. The design of these machines is essentially the same as that of machines built more than a hundred and fifty years ago. By adjusting the cutting machine and changing its three working dies, many different sizes and styles of nails can be made.

The first of the three dies, called the header punch, is a round length of steel with one end machined into a concave surface. This die forms the top of the head. The second, a pair of gripper dies, firmly grasps the wire and determines the shape of the bottom half of the head. The third die is a pair of cutters, which pinches off the wire into a point. There is a different set of dies for each size and style of nail.

The spindle of drawn wire is placed in front of a cutting machine. The point of the rod is fed into a device that contains a series of eight pairs of rollers. As the wire, which has been coiled up most of the time, passes between the rollers, it is straightened out.

The rod is then grasped by a feeder arm and pulled into the cutting machine. The feeder arm is adjusted to pull the exact length of wire necessary to form the style of nail desired. The feeder arm is retracted and the two halves of the gripper die are joined around the wire with great pressure. The wire fits precisely into a slot in the middle of the closed grippers. A series of holding grooves cut into this slot help prevent the nail from moving when the head is formed.

A precisely measured length of wire is left protruding in front of the joined grippers. This section of wire is smacked

A spindle of drawn wire is placed in front of each of these nail-cutting machines. The mechanism extending out from the first machine holds the rollers, which straighten the wire before it is formed into a nail. From the rollers, the wire feeds into the nail-forming dies just below the lever. After the nails are cut, they fall into pans on the floor. The machines have wooden boxes built around them to reduce the noise level in the cutting room.

Three dies form and cut each nail. The first die is the header punch, which flattens the top half of the head. The second is a set of gripper dies. The indentation that forms the bottom half of the head can be clearly seen on the left gripper. The ridges left by the grippers are below the head on the nail. The third is a pair of cutting dies, which point the nail.

by the header punch, forcing the steel into a round indentation machined into the face of the grippers. The diameter and thickness of the head are determined by the amount of wire protruding in front of the grippers and by the shape of the indentation.

The gripper dies leave two sets of marks on each nail. On the underside of the head, on opposite sides, are two thin ridges of steel. These are formed when the header punch pushes the steel between a thin space where the two halves of the gripper die come together. On the shank of the nail, below the head, is a series of other marks. These are also formed by the impact of the header punch, which pushes the steel into the holding grooves cut into the slot of the grippers.

As the header punch withdraws, the two cutter dies come together to slice off the other end of the wire into a point. The grippers then open and release the nail, which falls down a chute into a metal container below the machine. As soon as the nail is released, the feeder arm pulls another length of wire into the machine and the process is repeated. Smaller nails can be produced at a rate of nine hundred a minute while longer nails, up to 12 inches, are made at a rate of one hundred and forty a minute.

As the two cutting dies were joined to point and cut the nail, a thin sliver of steel, called a burr, escaped between the two halves of the dies. To remove this razor-sharp edge, the nails are brought to a tumbling machine. Thousands of nails, along with abrasive grit and sawdust, are placed in a large tank. As the tank is rotated, the nails bang against each other and knock off the burrs. The grit is added to give the nails a low luster, and the sawdust to absorb the lubricating soap used on the drawing machine.

After being tumbled for several hours, the nails are automatically emptied onto a conveyor belt with a vibrating screen. This separates the sawdust, grit, and burrs from the nails. The nails are then moved to the packaging area to be boxed or taken to other sections of the plant to be further processed.

A worker pours paint into a cement mixer containing nails. The nails receive an even coating of paint as the mixer rotates.

If the nails are going to be used in stone or concrete, for example, they are heat-treated to make them especially hard and strong. This is done by heating them until they are red-hot, quickly cooling them in oil or water, and then slowly reheating them. For use in wood paneling, some nails are painted to match the color of the wood. To retard steel nails from rusting, they may be coated with a hot zinc compound. These special nails are also packed in 50-pound boxes for shipping.

PLASTIC BOTTLES

An important aspect of the revolution in packaging has been the development of sophisticated methods for making plastic bottles. There are three general categories of bottles, each with its own manufacturing technologies. Each method leaves its own distinctive marks on the bottles, which easily identifies which process was used.

The *injection molding* method is used to make small bottles, for example, the vials in which prescription drugs are dispensed. These containers have a slightly smaller diameter at their base than their mouths. Their shape is cylindrical, with no curves or indentations. In the middle of the bottom of these bottles is a small circle, or halo. This is a gatemark, indicating where the melted plastic was injected into the mold when the bottle was made.

Small bottles, usually no larger than 8 ounces, with a curved shape are manufactured by the *injection blow molding* process. Small aspirin bottles with shoulders flaring out beneath the neck are made this way. A firm sometimes produces 100 million of these bottles a year. These containers also have the circular gatemark in the center of the bottom. In addition, they have a thin parting line that runs up both sides of the bottle.

Plastic bottles larger than 8 ounces that have a contoured shape or a handle are made by the *extrusion blow molding* method. These bottles, which have a neck or spout considerably smaller than the base, also have a parting line on the bottom and both sides.

An extrusion blow mold machine can produce more than

10 million gallon bottles a year, enough to bottle the petroleum pumped from all the oil wells in Oklahoma. Bottles so produced are usually made to a customer's specifications. Most job shops, firms that fill orders from many different customers, won't produce an order for fewer than 10,000 bottles. A perusal of the liquid detergent section of a supermarket attests to the great variety of sizes, styles, shapes, colors, and labeling methods of these bottles. There are over one hundred and fifty styles and shapes of 1-gallon bottles.

High- and low-density polyethylene, polystyrene, polypropylene, and polyvinyl chloride are common plastics used in the manufacturing of bottles. Each material has different characteristics. Stress, heat and chemical resistance, transparency, and, most important, cost are all factors considered when a bottle is designed.

A large percentage of the bottles produced by this method are made either from a high- or low-density polyethylene, a petroleum-derived plastic. The high-density plastic is strong and stiff, without much flexibility. Low-density plastic has a rubbery feel to it and is much more flexible. The alignment of the molecular structure in the polyethylene determines the density of the plastic. The more ordered and aligned the molecules, the less resistance the structure offers to distortion. Molecular structure that is askew offers more resistance.

Wooden gaylords filled with polyethylene pellets. The plastic tube in the gaylord on the right vacuums the pellets into the hopper of the blow molding machine at the far right.

Polyethylene is manufactured by chemical companies in pellet form, and the plastic is delivered to the bottle factory in railroad cars. A giant vacuum device sucks the pellets into large holding silos at the side of the building. From these storage silos, the pellets are poured into large portable wooden boxes called gaylords.

Gaylords full of pellets are placed beside the molding machines. If the finished bottle is going to be a color other than the natural, milky, translucent appearance of the polyethylene, colored dye pellets are mixed in at a precise ratio. A vacuum tube is placed in the gaylords to suck the pellets into a hopper on top of the molding machine.

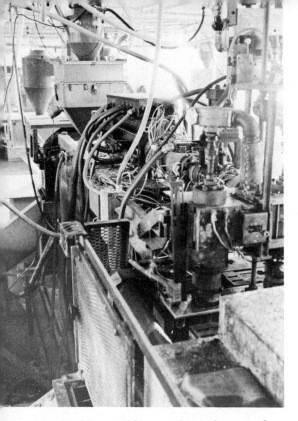

On this blow molding machine, the control panel is visible at the bottom left. The dies are located inside the screen gate.

This two-part mold shapes a soft tube of plastic into a quart bottle. The holes on the sides of the mold admit the cold water into the internal channels. The set screws, which hold the interchangeable threads in the mold, can be seen in the top center of each half of the mold.

The pellets are dropped into the barrel of the molding machine and heated to 450° F. It takes from three and a half to four minutes to transform the hard pellets into a soft, viscous state. In this form, the plastic, now called the melt, is moved by a twisting screw mechanism to the front of the machine.

Under great pressure from the screw, the melt is forced downward through a set of annular extruding dies to form a thin-walled tube, which is somewhat longer than the bottle being made. (See pages 53–54 for the explanation of how an annular die works.)

As soon as the tube is forced downward, two halves of an aluminum mold close around it. Inside each half of the mold is a hollow cavity the exact shape of half a bottle. When the mold is tightly clamped together, the cavity formed by the two halves takes the form of the bottle. As the mold closes, it pinches together the bottom inch of the hanging tube. The bottom is crimped like the bottom of a toothpaste tube. The mold also forces the soft plastic around the extruding dies. This forms an airtight seal at both ends of the tube.

Located in the center of the extruding die is a blow pin. Compressed air is released at a pressure of 2000 pounds per square inch (psi) through the blow pin into the sealed tube. This sudden rush of air blows the tube out evenly in all directions against the walls of the mold. The soft, pliable plastic adopts the exact, bottle-shaped form of the mold.

A thin seam or ridge, called the parting line, is formed around the bottle as small amounts of plastic escape between the two halves of the clamped mold. The seam is often much larger on the bottom of the bottle, where the mold pinched the tube together.

A series of channels built into the structure of the mold, behind the shaped cavity, allows cold water to be pumped in and circulated. Because the hot plastic is semisoft and easily deformed after it is blown, it is cooled while surrounded by the cold mold. It takes four seconds to extrude and blow the plastic tube and twenty seconds to cool the bottle. On hot, humid days, moisture forms between the inside of the cold mold and the hot plastic. This sweating, or condensation, causes a fine pebble effect on the surface of the bottle.

When the molding cycle is completed, the mold opens and releases the bottle onto a conveyor belt, which moves the bottles onto a series of cooling tiers. Because the bottles are warm and easily dented, they are slowly circulated around the wire tiers, allowing them to set-up to their final hardness.

After being extruded through the annular dies, the soft plastic tube hangs downward. The two halves of the mold, at the right and left, are about to close around it.

A technician examines bottles as they slowly circulate around the cooling tier. Extending from the top and bottom of the bottles are the flashings.

69

The bottles, which have been automatically tipped over onto a conveyor system, are about to have the flashing cut off. The fine threads of plastic hanging from the screen are produced when the drill smoothes the inside of the spout.

Protruding from both the bottom and top of the formed bottles are finlike pieces of polyethylene called flashing. The bottom flashing is the part of the tube pinched together when the mold closed and is called the tail. The top flashing is the excess forced around the extruding die just above the spout of the bottle. These will become scrap material.

After cooling for several minutes, the bottles are automatically fed from the tiers through a series of secondary operations. They are automatically tipped over onto their sides on another conveyor belt, and as they move along, a pair of guillotine knives cuts off the tail. Another pair of knives cuts off the top flashing above the threads on the spout. The bottles then pass beside an automatic drill, which advances into the spout to smooth off any inside rough edges.

The kind of cap that goes on a plastic bottle is determined by the product it holds. For instance, a gallon bottle of distilled water takes a simple screw-on cap. A bottle of antifreeze requires a more secure lock-on type of closure. If a cap loosens on a bottle in a supermarket display, the leaking antifreeze would be much more ruinous to other products on the shelves than the distilled water. Each type of cap requires a different thread on the spout of the bottle, and there are as many as ten different thread styles used on a 1-gallon bottle.

Instead of having to make a completely different mold for each different thread style, blow molding firms design the molds with interchangeable threads. If the antifreeze company orders the same style 1-gallon bottle as the distilled water bottler, a single mold can be used for both. The two $\frac{1}{2}$-inch sections of grooved and curved steel that form the threads for the screw-on cap are unbolted from the two halves of the mold. These are replaced with the lock-on type of mold threads.

The decoration or labeling on a bottle can be applied in several ways, depending on how much money the customer wants to spend. Printed paper labels can be glued on, or a printed plastic sleeve can be semiautomatically slipped over

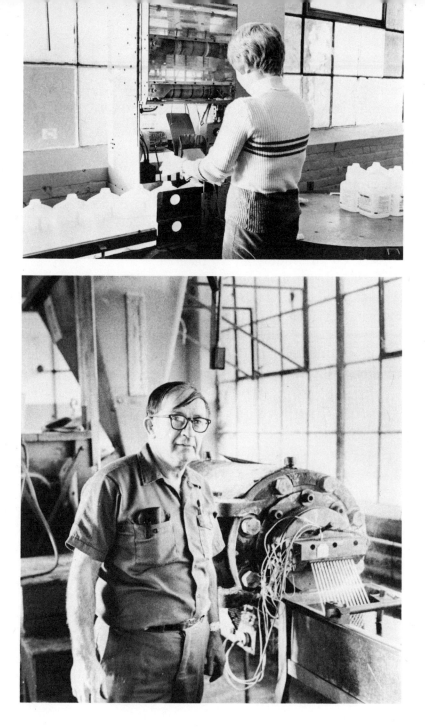

The bottles are moved by conveyor belt to one of the labeling machines. A worker slips a printed plastic sleeve, automatically dispensed by the machine in front of her, over each bottle. From the platform on the right, the labeled bottles are moved to the packing room.

Scrap plastic generated from the bottle-making process is ground up and poured into the barrel of the machine behind the worker. The plastic is melted and extruded in fourteen continuous streams. These can be seen entering the cooling bath, which solidifies the plastic. After leaving the bath, the plastic passes beneath chopping blades, which reduce the plastic to pieces the size of the original pellets. These recycled pellets are then reintroduced into the blow molding machine.

the bottle. The application of heat transfer inks and silk-screening are more expensive processes. These methods print the graphics directly onto the surface of the bottle in several colors.

After receiving their labels, the bottles are strapped together on wooden pallets, wrapped in thin, clear plastic sheets for protection, and loaded onto railroad cars or trailer trucks for shipping. Because of the cost of shipping the empty bottles, most manufacturers don't supply customers outside a 350-mile radius of their plant.

Extrusion blow molding is a process ideally suited to the mass production of plastic household liquid containers. However, it is interesting to note that a company in Europe, where packaging technology is more innovative, is experimenting with the same method for making 350-gallon plastic oil fuel tanks for single-family homes.

FOAM RUBBER

A day doesn't pass without most people sitting on a seat made of synthetic foam rubber—all automobile seats and most cushions for chairs and sofas are manufactured from polyurethane foam. Originally, foam rubber was made from natural latex produced from rubber trees. After the Second World War, synthetic latex, called styrene-butadiene rubber (SBR), replaced the natural foam; now polyurethane is the most commonly used material for foam products. It is a low-cost, petroleum-derived plastic and has many other uses as well.

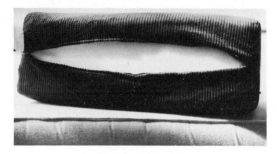

Chemically, the production of polyurethane is a tricky business that entails hundreds of possible formulations. In the industry it is said that polyurethane is like wood — it has a thousand uses. By varying the chemicals and the way they are mixed, polyurethane can be flexible, as in seat cushions; semiflexible, as in skateboard wheels or rubber bumpers on new cars; or rigid, like the hard heels on women's high-heeled shoes.

In many ways, the production of foam rubber is like baking. In making a cake, a baker mixes flour, eggs, baking powder, and milk. The reaction in a heated oven between the lactic acid in the milk and the sodium bicarbonate in the baking powder, which is alkaline, produces carbon dioxide (CO_2) and water. The CO_2, expanding under heat, forms bubblelike cells in the flour and egg mixture. As the bubbles expand, the dough rises. When the temperature reaches the right level, the gas escapes by bursting the walls of the cells, leaving a threadlike network of baked flour. By changing the proportions of the ingredients, a baker can vary the consistency from the density of a pound cake to the lightness of angel food.

Foam rubber is produced by two chemical reactions occurring simultaneously. Gas is produced, trapped, and expanded as huge polymer carbon and hydrogen molecules link up to form the plastic polyurethane network. As in the cake, gas bubbles expand in a liquid mixture, which then solidifies into a porous form.

Polyurethane, which corresponds to the flour and egg mixture in the cake, has a molecular structure that can be viewed as a two-dimensional ladder. The sides of the ladder are long chains of polyol molecules, and the rungs, or links, are toluene diisocyanate (TDI). If there are only a few rungs to hold the ladder together, it will be flexible and shaky. A strong ladder will have many rungs. The thickness of the sides of the ladder is determined by the molecular weight of the polyol, and the number of connecting rungs determines the strength or tearability of the polyurethane foam. The process of linking the polyol and TDI molecules to form the ladder and interconnecting enormous numbers of these in three dimensions is called polymerization.

If polyol and TDI are mixed together and put aside to cure, or harden, for several days, the result is a solid piece of polyurethane. But if water is added when the polyol and TDI are mixed, heat and gas are produced. Just as in making a cake, CO_2 bubbles are formed and expand because of the heat.

When the gas bubbles form, they are trapped between the linked molecules. As they expand, they separate the molecular ladders, causing the mixture to foam and expand. By controlling the amount of bubbling, called blowing, chemical engineers can determine how dense the foam will be. A foam with a very low density, one that can be squeezed very easily, is made by producing great numbers of CO_2 bubbles. The density of foam rubber determines its softness and is measured in pounds per cubic feet. The foam commonly used in seat cushions weighs 1.3 pounds per cubic foot. If a line 1 inch long were measured on this foam, there would be fifty to sixty cells on it. (A cell is the solidified polyurethane wall of the bubbles after the gas has escaped.) By volume, this foam would have about nine parts of air to every part of polyurethane.

The measurement of the spring tension, or load-bearing quality, of foam rubber is called the indentation load deflection (ILD) and reflects the number and strength of the interconnected chemical ladders of the polyurethane. The ILD scale is determined by the amount of weight it takes to compress a circle of foam by 25 percent. The area of this circle is 50 square inches, the size of the average buttocks, and is 4 inches thick. Most seat-cushioning foam has a rating of 35 ILD; that is, it takes 35 pounds of pressure to compress the 4-inch foam 1 inch.

For production purposes, several other chemicals are added to the polyol and TDI mixture. Tin and amines are added as catalysts, to speed up and coordinate the gas development and molecular growth. The reactions are controlled to trap the gas efficiently at the same time that the polyurethane network begins to stabilize. Liquid freon or methylene chloride gas is added as an additional blowing agent to increase the number of bubbles produced, surfactants to control the size of the bubbles, and liquid silicone to help stabilize the cell structure. If the foam is to be colored other than its natural white, a dye is added. If it is being produced to meet fire codes, a fire-retardant chemical is added.

Most foams consist of 50 percent polyol, 40 percent TDI, and 10 percent water and other chemicals. The molecular structure, amount, and temperature of each ingredient determine the characteristics and subsequent use of the foam.

Because foam rubber is a bulk product, it requires buildings that are often 100 yards long, called pouring plants, for its manufacture. The liquid chemicals are delivered either by railroad tanker cars or tank trucks and pumped into large

The round heated mixing tank is in the background. In front of it is the square, black control panel that regulates metered pumps, which force the chemicals through a series of pipes and hoses to the mixing head off to the right.

holding tanks outside the plant. From there the chemicals are pumped into smaller heated mixing tanks. Chemicals that react with each other are kept in separate tanks.

To produce the foam, a plant needs a set of metered pumps, chemical-resistant hoses, plastic sheeting, a mixing head, and a conveyor belt almost as long as the building.

Above each side of the conveyor belt is a track system of holding clips. The clips move at the same speed as the conveyor belt, 15 feet a minute. An 8-inch roll of plastic

sheeting is placed horizontally on a dispenser in front of the mixing head. The plastic sheeting is the same kind that is stapled to the windows of houses as insulation during the winter. As the sheet is unrolled, it passes under the mixing head, and its sides are clipped onto the track system. This bends the plastic into a U shape, with the bottom of the U resting on the conveyor belt below the mixing head.

A specific amount of each chemical, measured by the metered pumps, is fed from the mixing tanks through the hoses into the mixing head. This head, a hollow barrel with a dispensing nozzle, spins at 4000 rpm 4 inches above the bottom of the plastic U. As the head spins, thoroughly blending the chemicals, it passes back and forth in a fixed line over the width of the conveyor belt.

As the head continuously passes across the conveyor belt, it pours a ¼-inch-deep layer of chemicals onto the bottom

Here the plastic sheeting enters the front of the foaming machine. The foaming head is the small, white vertical shape just to the right of the center of the photograph and to the left of the little black hood.

77

A worker clips one side of the plastic sheeting onto the track system to form the U into which the foam is poured. He is wearing a respirator to prevent his inhaling the noxious fumes released by the chemical toluene diisocyanate (TDI).

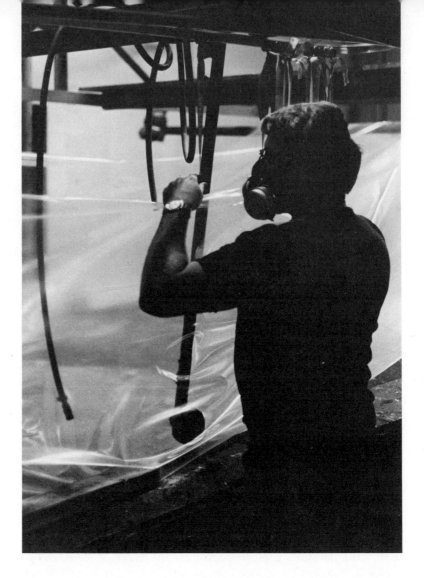

of the moving plastic U. The chemical reactions begin immediately. Within 2 feet of the pour line, the polymerization, heat generation, and gas blowing begin. The polyurethane foam rises and expands while contained within the U-shaped plastic sheet. In less than a minute it reaches a height of 24 inches.

As the foam moves down the conveyor belt, the CO_2, which has been trapped in the cells of polyurethane, bursts through the polyurethane walls and begins to escape. About 10 percent of the weight of the combined chemicals is lost

The mixing head, at the lower right of the photograph, is covered with a special cloth to promote the even distribution of the mixture. The head moves back and forth across the bottom of the U. At the right and left are the clips holding up the plastic sheeting, which contains the poured foam. The foam can be seen rising a few feet in front of the mixing head.

in this way. If the catalysts have acted properly, the polymerization will have sufficiently solidified the structures of the cell walls so they remain in the foamed configuration once the gas has escaped. The heat generated by the reaction between the water and TDI, which produced the expanded CO_2 bubbles, brings the internal temperature of the foam to 280°–300° F.

When the mixing head first begins laying down the chemicals, it may produce an uneven mixture. As a result, about the first 20 feet of foam are unstable. This instability often produces excess heat. Routinely, the first section of foam is taken out of the plant and put into a metal cage, and after several hours it often bursts into flames. Because of the high potential for fires, pouring plants are required to have special insurance and double sprinkler systems.

The chemicals for the first 20 feet of foam are not blended properly by the mixing head. Several workers, wearing protective plastic gloves, hold up the front of this batch of foam and guide it along the conveyor belt. Highly flammable, it will be taken outside.

The stream of foam, which has risen to 24 inches, passes below the horizontal band saw at right. The saw, which is behind the flexible vent, is synchronized to descend and cut 12-foot sections as the foam moves along the conveyor belt.

After they have been cut by the band saw in the background, the buns are carried toward the curing area by the conveyor belt.

The mixing head pours the chemicals at a rate of about 500 pounds per minute; when foamed, they form enough polyurethane to fill a 40-foot trailer truck in three minutes. As the foam moves toward the end of the conveyor belt, it passes under a horizontal band saw. The saw is timed to descend and cut the continuous stream of foam in 12-foot sections, called buns, for easy handling. If the foam were not cut to be cured and stored, the mixing machine could pour a continuous ribbon of foam rubber 4 or 5 miles long in a seven-hour workday.

If the foam is poured in the afternoon, the buns usually have to be cured overnight. They must be laid out on their bottoms rather than stacked because the cell structure of the foam is not yet firm enough to withstand any accumulated weight. After this curing period, the buns are ready to be cut into seat cushions, mattresses, soft toilet seats, filters, stuffing for pincushions, toys, packaging, or a thousand other uses.

The buns are brought to a second band saw to be cut into mattresses or other foam products. The self-sharpening saw revolves around the platform and cuts the buns to the thickness desired. After each rotation, the blade is automatically lowered to a pre-set height and repeats the cutting operation.

BRICKS

Brick is the oldest manufactured building material. Archaeological excavations have unearthed bricks that are more than nine thousand years old. The history of the art of brickmaking parallels the growth and expansion of the ancient Egyptian, Assyrian, Chinese, and Roman civilizations. This manufacturing heritage, so closely entwined with architecture, both historical and contemporary, is based on a material formed in prehistoric times.

Clay, the raw material for bricks, was formed tens of thousands of years ago by glacial action or by weathering, both of which reduced rocks and pebbles to fine particles. Most of the brick used is produced from clay deposits left during one of the four glacial periods. The earlier these deposits were laid down, the more pressure they received from succeeding layers, producing a solid, dry, almost rocklike clay. Deposits of clay that were formed later under less pressure are moist and plastic.

The age or fineness of the clay, the amount of water it contains, and its mineral organic composition are all crucial factors in brickmaking. They determine the manufacturing processes, the appearance of the brick, and, ultimately, how it will be used. Clays differ dramatically in composition from sites less than 200 miles apart. This difference could necessitate completely different brickmaking processes.

The particle size and water content of the clay determine the brick-forming process, and the mineral content, to a large extent, the color of the brick. All of these factors dictate the drying and baking procedures that harden the clay.

The brickmaker's sensitivity to these differences, which can vary even at one clay pit, is why brickmaking is considered an art.

The many brick-forming processes fall into two very general categories: clay can be extruded like toothpaste out of a tube and then cut into the desired shapes, or it can be pressed into a mold to determine its shape. The extrusion method is better for drier, coarser clay and is used by highly automated firms producing a high-volume product in a few standard sizes. Firms in the United States using this method produce 935 million bricks a year. The molding method is a more old-fashioned, specialized process suitable for a wetter, finer clay. A typical firm using the molding process will make about 20 million bricks a year in many different sizes, shapes, and colors.

The factory shown in the photographs uses the molding process for clay that has a very fine, wet composition (30 percent water) and a high iron content (5 percent). The clay formed during the last glacial period is excellent for this process. One acre of this clay 1 foot deep makes 1 million bricks.

The clay is dug out of the clay pit by a power shovel and taken by dump truck to the brickworks, a short distance away. In examining the deposits in the clay pit, one can

Before 1907, when the steam shovel was invented, all clay was dug by hand. The clay being dug up here will be delivered from the clay pit by truck to the brickworks, several hundred yards away.

After being dumped by the truck onto a conveyor belt, the clay is moved up and deposited into the pug mill in the background, below the top of the conveyor belt. The pug mill churns the clay and other ingredients together. To the right of the pug mill is the brick-forming machine.

see ⅛-inch-thick layers or bands of slightly different colors. These bands mark the summers and winters of the glacial period.

The clay is dumped from the truck into a holding container and moved by conveyor belt to the pug mill, where it is mixed with other materials. The pug mill has a series of rotating blades that churn the clay and other ingredients together for forty minutes.

If, for example, a particular load of clay is too moist, washed and dried sand is added to firm up the consistency. The sand is first cleaned to eliminate unwanted minerals, which would turn the brick an unplanned color. Other materials can be added to determine the final color of the brick: powdered iron to make clay with a low iron content turn redder, lampblack or ash for an artificial black appearance, kaolin clay for a light- or tan-colored brick, talc or a special solution to make the salt in the clay insoluble for a powdery white effect on a red brick.

After the clay has been mixed, it is ready to be molded. Each kind of clay requires a different wood mold because of the different moisture content and fineness of the clay particles. The molds at this firm are made of cherry, which, when wet, expands evenly in all directions. Molds also come in different shapes. Often an architect or builder will order spe-

This cherrywood mold is made by the only brick mold maker in the United States. There is no single, standard-sized brick. Each brick that comes from this mold will have the initials of the brickmaker on the side.

85

This hydraulic press, which receives the clay directly from the pug mill, was built in the early part of the century. Empty molds enter the press on a roller system, seen in the lower section of the machine. After the clay is forced into the mold, it passes under a metal scraper that removes any excess clay from the top to form the smooth face of the brick. The filled molds, seen below the handle, are automatically removed from the press.

cial bricks, for instance, ones with rounded corners, which require their own custom-built mold. There is only one mold maker in the United States.

Each mold contains seven brick-sized sections into which the clay is forced by a hydraulic press under several tons' pressure. After the mold has been filled, it passes under a metal scraper, which removes the excess clay from the surface. It is moved to the end of the press and flipped over.

Once it is upside down, the mold is jiggled and banged on the side by an automatic hammer. This knocks the bricks free and onto metal trays. (Every twenty minutes the molds are soaked in water so that the clay won't stick to them when the bricks are removed.) Once the mold is empty, it is automatically returned to the front of the press to\repeat the brickmaking procedure.

After the bricks have been molded, they are ready to be dried and fired. These procedures are also varied, depending on the type of clay and source of heat. In pre-industrial processes, practiced in warm climates, bricks are dried outside for several days and then piled into a tunnel-like structure. Wood or charcoal is placed inside and lit, and the fire bakes the clay. Modern methods are either the continuous system, in which the bricks are constantly kept in motion as they pass through a heating chamber, or the batch system, in which the bricks are piled 20 feet high on a special platform in a kiln.

The filled molds are automatically lifted from the top of the press (out of the picture to the left), flipped over, and banged by automatic hammers to knock the formed bricks onto flat steel shelves. These two workers control the mold press and constantly watch a closed-circuit TV, top right, to make sure there are no jam-ups on any part of the manufacturing line.

In the foreground, empty steel trays are returning to the press to be loaded again. Workers in the background pile dried bricks that are ready for the kiln.

At this factory, the metal trays full of bricks are placed on moving racks that run on a small rail system. These "cars" move the bricks slowly through a large closed room, called the drying chamber, for thirty-six hours. The temperature increases from 110° to about 300° F as the cars move through the dryer. Because of the evaporation of the moisture in the clay, the bricks, which may originally be 9⅛ inches long, shrink to 8½ inches. They come out of the dryer firm but easily breakable and have turned from their initial gray color to a soft grayish red. It is not unknown for karate schools to obtain brick for their breaking exercises from this stage in the brickmaking process.

The brick is removed from the dryer and piled up in a special formation on pallets. This arrangement leaves passages, or channels, between the bricks to promote heat circulation while they are being fired. Once on the pallets, the bricks are taken by fork-lift truck to the kilns.

Batch-type kilns heated by oil are used to fire the brick in this factory. The use of these domed kilns is an old-fashioned method, but has certain advantages over more high-volume ones. Heat and oxygen, which are pumped into the

From the molding machine, the bricks are placed on metal trays, which are then loaded onto these steel racks, or cars, mounted on rails. These units move through a continuous drying oven.

The bricks are taken from the drying ovens, allowed to cool, and put onto a conveyor belt. These workers, stationed along the conveyor belt, remove the bricks and place them in a special formation on a movable platform called a pallet. They are arranged with open channels running through the pile to allow heat to circulate as they are being fired in the kiln.

89

The bricks are brought to one of these domed oil-heated kilns to be baked to their rocklike consistency.

enclosed chamber, can be precisely controlled. By varying these two factors, the colors of the brick can be controlled. After several days in the kiln, the temperature approaches 1900° F, and the iron in the clay begins to oxidize, becoming ferrous oxide. This turns the brick orange.

Because the heat and air are being pumped in from above, those bricks closer to the heat source are subjected to higher temperatures. The more heat a brick receives, the larger the percentage of iron in the clay that oxidizes. The increased heat also fuses the clay particles together. Therefore, these bricks will be stronger and turn red. Those bricks farther from the high temperatures will be light orange and weaker, with a rough, porous texture. Often, as you can see when an old brick building is torn down, the center of the walls was made of the more common orange brick, which

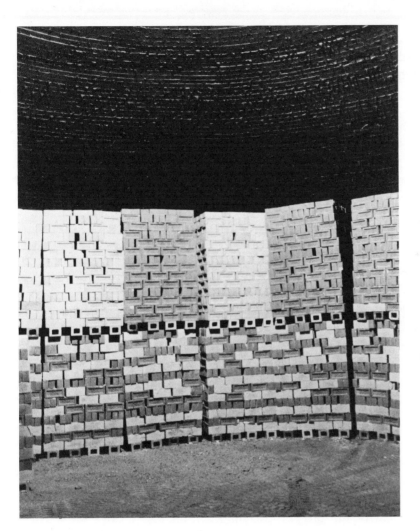

The bricks are piled up inside the kiln. Here there are some light-colored bricks made from kaolin clay along with the more usual type of brick. This clay, purchased from a clay pit in a nearby state, contains no iron to turn the brick red.

received the least amount of heat. The surface of the building was made out of the face brick, which is darker, stronger, and has better weather-resistant qualities.

If the air being pumped into the kiln is shut off and the heat increased to 1930°–1950° F, the brick will begin to turn a shiny black-red. This signifies that the iron has completely oxidized and that the particles of clay have all fused together. This darkened, partially black brick, which is called vitreous, is often used for paving roads and sidewalks

This machine, called a carousel, revolves as workers place the finished bricks in separate compartments according to the color pattern specified by the purchaser.

because it can withstand the effects of ice, snow, and abrasion.

After the bricks have been in the kiln for 120 hours, the heat is shut off. The original 9⅛-inch-long brick has further shrunk to 7¾ inches. The bricks are allowed to cool and then moved outside. If the face of a building is to be a solid dark red, then only those bricks closest to the heat in each of the kilns will be used. If a mixture of colors is desired, a device called a carousel is used. Workers located around the rotating carousel will take bricks that are different colors and place one of each color into the compartments as they pass around.

When the compartments are filled with the desired number and mixture of bricks, they are removed, banded to-

The bricks are banded together, in different ways for the convenience of each masonry contractor, and loaded on a flatbed trailer. These trucks have special hoists, or booms, that allow the packaged bricks to be carefully unloaded at the building site. This rather small, specialized brickyard produces 20 million bricks a year, enough to cover the surface of Vermont and Massachusetts.

gether, and taken by fork lift to a flatbed masonry delivery vehicle. This truck has a specially designed lifting device, called a boom, that lowers the bricks to the ground at the construction site.

ASPHALT CONCRETE

The official name for the material commonly called asphalt or blacktop is bituminous or asphalt concrete. Some 91 percent of all American roads and highways are surfaced with this material. These roadways, if connected, would stretch around the earth seventy-three times. Often 25 inches thick, they function as a protective layer for the earth below. Ultimately, it is the graded surface of the earth that carries the traffic load.

Before highway engineers design a roadway, they determine how many and what kind of vehicles are going to use it. They must predict the maximum loads of trucks and cars, how often these vehicles will use the roads, and the supporting capacity of the soil beneath the roadbed. The load-bearing characteristics of the soil largely determine the thickness and composition of the asphalt road. Some soils, such as rocky or coarse-grained sandy soils, are strong and can bear up under great pressure. Clay and fine-grained soils decompose relatively fast and cannot effectively support great weights.

When the road use is determined — for example, either by heavy trucks on an Interstate or by light traffic on a secondary road — the engineers design a road structure that will be economical to build and maintain. This structure is flexible and designed to distribute the high-intensity weight and stress of the traffic load downward and outward to the earth below.

Roads are constructed out of several layers, or courses, of asphalt concrete; each one has a different composition and thickness. The courses are made of a mixture of sand and different sizes of crushed stone or gravel, called aggregate, which is imbedded in asphalt. By varying the relative amounts of these materials, engineers control a road's stability, skid resistance, durability, and effectiveness in preventing water infiltration.

An Interstate almost always is constructed of three courses, with a total height of 13 inches, laid on top of a 12-inch-thick foundation of gravel. Secondary roads usually have two courses, with a height of $5\frac{1}{4}$ inches. These two layers also rest upon a foot-thick gravel foundation. The load-bearing qualities of a roadway are determined by the strength and thickness of the lower courses.

As a truck tire passes over a spot on the pavement, the stress and weight are absorbed by the most flexible top course. This spot on the road, directly below each tire of a moving vehicle, is deformed and deflected downward into the stronger courses below. When the vehicle passes, the spot on the pavement returns to its original shape. The second and third layers, which are both stronger and not as flexible, absorb the weight and stress and spread them downward and out through the road structure and into the earth.

The crushed quarry stone imbedded in the asphalt is the material that actually transfers the weight and stress. The sizes of the stone in the aggregate range from $\frac{1}{4}$ inch to $1\frac{1}{2}$ inches in diameter. Stronger courses consist of a low percentage of small stones and a higher percentage of large sizes. Quarry stone, which is fractured and angular, is used because the flat faces of the stones fit together evenly and give the aggregate strength under pressure. The stress from the weight of a moving vehicle passes from each stone to the next one it is in contact with below.

Pebbles and gravel, which are less expensive than quarry stone, are sometimes substituted for it. The rounded shape of these materials doesn't afford as many areas of contact between their surfaces. Consequently, the few points that are in contact bear more of the pressure, thus preventing a strong body in the asphalt mixture. Roads made of pebbles and gravel require much more repair and maintenance because of this inefficiency in absorbing the weight of the passing traffic. A roadway made of these materials tends to crack, fray, and disintegrate rapidly.

Quarry stone is produced by drilling and blasting a rock ledge into large chunks. These are placed in a primary crusher, which breaks them up into smaller pieces. They are then passed through a series of secondary crushers and sieve screens. The system progressively reduces and separates out the desired sizes of stone. As many as four or five different sizes can be produced by the same quarry.

The asphalt used in modern roads is a black residue left when the volatile substances, gas and oil, are distilled, or fractioned, from crude petroleum. When heated, asphalt is soft and viscous; when cooled, it hardens and acts like glue to bind other materials together. Sand and dust from the broken stone are used in the mixture to help fill the small pockets of air, called voids, formed between the aggregate-in-asphalt mixture.

The top, or third, layer of a road is usually $1\frac{1}{2}$ inches deep and is called the finish, or wearing, course. It contains the greatest percentage of asphalt. It consists of approximately 60 percent fine aggregate (sand, dust, and stones no bigger than $\frac{1}{4}$ inch in diameter), 34 percent coarse aggregate (stone ranging from $\frac{3}{4}$ inch to $1\frac{1}{2}$ inches in diameter), and 6 percent asphalt. The finish course is the costliest layer to produce because of the expense of crushing stone into fine aggregate. This layer effectively resists abrasion and wear from vehicle traffic while acting as a seal against water. It provides a smooth and quiet ride because of the fineness of its composition.

If a road is designed for heavy traffic, a bottom, or base, course, which is the strongest, is put down directly above the gravel foundation. Spread throughout this 8-inch layer are many voids. These are created because there is a small percentage of fine aggregate and sand to fill up the spaces between the large stones. If the finish course were laid directly on this base coat, the weight of the traffic would cause it to be compressed into the voids of the base course. If this happened, the road surface would begin to decompose.

To prevent this filtering effect, a second, or binder, course, 4 inches thick, is sandwiched between the finish and base course. This layer, intermediate in strength, has an even distribution of fine and coarse aggregate. It has stones large enough to prevent it from being forced into the voids of the base course. It also has a high enough percentage of fine aggregate to keep the top coat from sinking into it. On secondary roads it is the binder course that gives the roadway its strength. Because great strength is not necessary on these roads, only the top two courses are laid over the gravel foundation.

Below the base course is a 12-inch gravel foundation, called the sub-base. This layer acts as a supporting foundation for the road. It also provides a drainage system that prevents any underground water from permeating the asphalt courses. Such water would cause erosion and deterioration of the road. Below the sub-base is the subgrade, the prepared and compacted soil of the earth.

Bituminous concrete is manufactured at a hot mix plant. It is an outdoor process that requires masses of materials, automated moving equipment, and few workers. The sand and various sizes of quarry stone are delivered by dump trailer trucks and deposited in a holding or storage yard. The asphalt is delivered by tank trucks and pumped into storage tanks.

The sand and stone are moved by bulldozer from the holding yard and dumped into a series of feed bins, or chutes. The chutes, which act as funnels, have a volume control valve that feeds the materials onto a conveyor belt in a tunnel below. A worker in the tunnel controls the amount of sand and of the different-sized aggregates that are poured onto the moving belt. Called the primary mix,

Asphalt, a petroleum product, is delivered by trucks and stored in these tanks. Each tank can hold 7000 gallons.

Sand and the various sizes of aggregate are delivered by truck and dumped into the holding yard.

A bulldozer, moving at top speed, scoops the sand and aggregate from separate piles and dumps them into a series of feed chutes.

The chutes, which act as funnels, have a volume flow control valve that feeds the materials onto a conveyor belt in a tunnel below. A worker in the tunnel controls the amount of sand and the proportion of different-sized aggregate that is poured onto the moving belt. This is called the primary mix.

this is rapidly conveyed up a ramp and through an oil-fueled burner, or heating system. The sand and aggregate are heated to 300°–350° F. Any moisture, which would prevent a good bind of materials in the final mix, is burned off here.

As soon as the materials leave the burner, a vacuum device sucks up the sand and dust through a series of pipes and deposits them in a holding bin located several stories up in the mixing structure. These will be returned later to the final mixture. The rest of the materials are transported by a heated elevator to a screening apparatus, also on the

The mixture of sand and aggregate is dumped from the conveyor belt at right onto a steep moving ramp that leads up to the top of a heating cylinder called the burner.

The sand and aggregate are quickly moved through this cylindrical burner on a special heat-resistant conveyor belt system.

mixing structure. This apparatus uses a series of vibrating screens to separate the hot aggregate by size into individual holding bins. There are four bins, one for the sand and stone dust, three for the different-sized stones.

An operator, who sits at a control console in a shack next to the mixing structure, determines what combination of materials will go into the final mix. He follows the course specification, called the job mix formula, supplied by the highway engineer. The appropriate amount, by weight, of each size of stone and sand is released from the holding bins and falls into a weigh box below. By changing the materials in the final mix, an asphalt plant can alter the product from a base course to a finish course in less than five minutes.

The aggregate is moved from the burner (lower left, background) by a heated elevator to the top of the mixing structure. A series of vibrating screens separates the stone, by size, into individual holding bins at the top.

An operator, sitting at a control console in a shack next to the mixing structure, determines what proportion of the sand and aggregate will go into the final mix. These are automatically weighed out, by the scale at the left, and dropped into the pub mill, or mixing box. A precise amount of asphalt is injected into the mill.

101

At the bottom of the mixing structure, the 300°–350° F mixture is released in a steamy mass into a buggy below. The shack housing the control panel is to the left.

When the right proportion of each material is weighed out, the operator activates the switch that releases the mixture into a pub mill, or mixing box. While the sand, dust, and stones are being thoroughly combined, asphalt is injected into the mill and mixed in for forty-five seconds.

The lumpy asphalt mixture, which has remained at about 350° F because of the heated aggregate, is then released in a steamy mass into a waiting cart, or buggy, below the pub mill. Each batch weighs 3 tons, enough to cover one lane of a highway for 15 yards at a 1-inch depth. It takes from three to five minutes from the time the aggregate is first put onto the conveyor belt at the feed chutes for it to be deposited in the buggy.

The buggy is automatically pulled up a steep ramp. When it reaches the top, it is flipped upside down, dumping the hot mix into one of three storage bins, one for each course. Asphalt dump trucks arrive at the plant and drive under one of the storage containers to receive a load. The hot asphalt mixture, which can remain in the truck for half a day before hardening, is then hauled to the road site. From the dump truck the asphalt concrete is fed into a mechanical spreader, which applies a smooth layer on the road that is then compacted by rollers. While the mixture is still hot and pliable, the compression from the roller packs the aggregate closely and thus creates a strong pavement.

The color of a roadway often varies from mile to mile — perhaps from a light gray to a reddish or even bluish hue. When it is first laid down, the asphalt concrete is a consistent black color. As the abrasion of passing tires wears off the asphalt, the quarry stone becomes partially exposed.

Because a single quarry can't produce enough stone to supply an asphalt concrete plant, the manufacturer will purchase stone from several different companies. Although these quarries are sometimes within a 30-mile radius of each other, they often crush different kinds of stone. Quartzite, basalt, limestone, and hornfels are commonly used rock, and

The buggy, at the top of the photograph, is mechanically pulled up a steep ramp. When it reaches the top, it is flipped upside down, dumping the hot mix into one of the three large storage bins. Asphalt dump trucks arrive at the plant and drive under one of the storage containers to receive a load.

all have varying colors depending on their mineral impurities. It is the different batches of stone in the finish course that account for the various hues of road surfaces.

A light gray surface on a roadway indicates that the asphalt in the finish course has oxidized with age. Oxidation, the same process that rusts steel, causes the asphalt to become stiff, which makes the finish course wear out rapidly. Road engineers estimate that they must resurface a highway every four or five years, for they have determined that the finish course wears down about ¼ inch a year.

EYEGLASS FRAMES

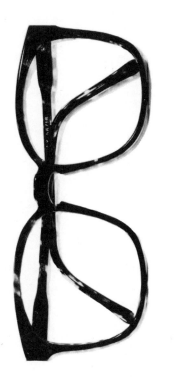

Eyeglasses are currently a stylish accessory that have changed from a necessity for a few to a fashion for many. The production of frames falls into two general categories. The sunglasses sold in a drugstore or notions store are mass-produced, using a molding process. They have noncorrective lenses, of either plastic or glass, are relatively inexpensive, and are not made to last a long time. The prescription glasses sold by an optometrist, worn by people who need corrective lenses, are usually die-cut from sheets of plastic. This process takes much hand labor and careful attention and produces a high-quality product with fine dimensional accuracy for a good fit.

The average firm producing frames by the die-cut method makes about fifteen thousand frames a week, almost enough in one year to supply every accountant in the United States with a pair of glasses. The frames are made in thirty-five styles in a variety of colors. Cellulose acetate, a cotton-derived plastic with both flexibility and strength, is the material from which the frames are made. The acetate, which is purchased in sheet form from a plastic manufacturer, is ordered by size, style, and color. To avoid wasting material when the frames are cut from the sheets, the frame maker buys them only a little wider than the width of the frames. The lengths of the sheets vary from 1½ to 3 feet long and are ⅓ inch thick.

The plastic is brought from a storage area to the blanking room. A sheet is placed in a small oven and heated for several minutes at 180° F. When it is taken out, it is semi-

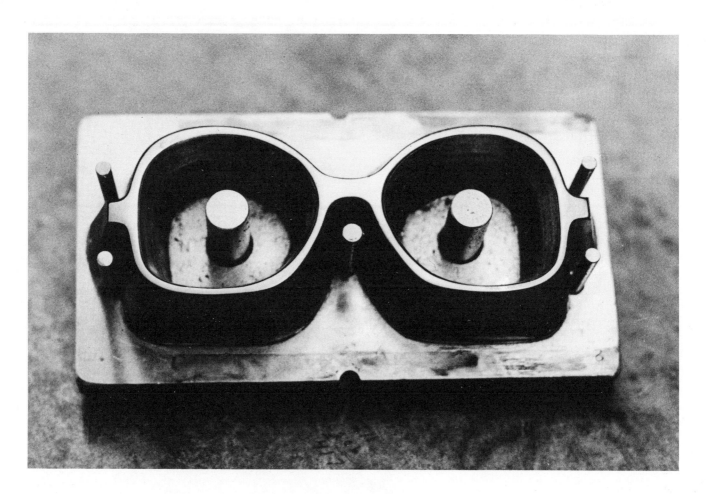

soft and would droop over the edge of a table. The heated sheet is immediately inserted into the blanking machine, which uses a steel rule die to cut out the frames, or blanks. The die is the shape of the frame and has razor-sharp edges. The machine operator releases a mechanism that forces the die through the plastic with several tons' pressure. The die is automatically lifted, the sheet moved up a little, and the process repeated. The last blanks on the sheet have to be stamped out quickly before the plastic cools and becomes too brittle to be cut.

The blanks are separated from the sheet after it is removed from the blanking machine. The portion where the lens will eventually fit is removed from the frame blank.

This steel rule die is used in the blanking machine to cut out the frame fronts. The inside and outside edges are razor sharp. Between them, white cushioning material, recessed ⅛ inch, is visible. The two large protruding rods help loosen the cut sections of the fronts, which are removed and later replaced with the corrective lenses.

After being heated in an oven, semisoft sheets of plastic are inserted into this blanking machine. A steel rule die is bolted into a holding fixture to the left of the lamp. An operator activates a switch, which forces the die downward through the plastic sheet. Scrap lens blanks that have been removed from the frame fronts can be seen on the floor.

This part becomes plastic scrap. The frame fronts, which are sharp-edged flat skeletons, are taken to the finishing room, where a series of secondary operations is performed. First, grooves are routered out of the inside of the frame where the lens will be inserted. The ⅛-inch wide grooves are standard for all prescription lenses. Even very thick lenses are ground down along the edges to fit into the smaller groove.

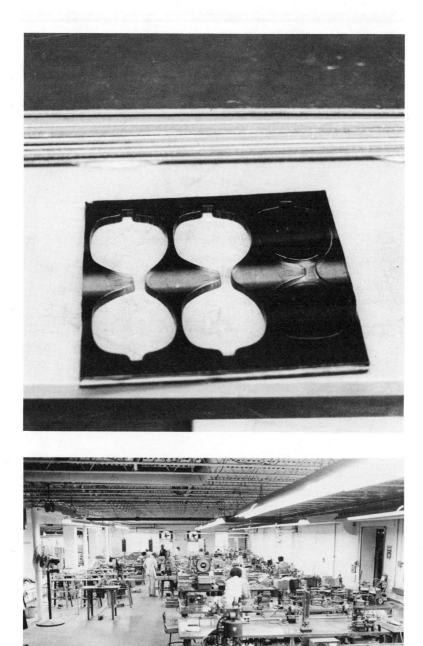

On the right side of this die-cut sheet is a frame front with the lens section still in place.

The fronts are brought to the finishing room, where several operations are performed.

One of the finishing operations cuts two grooves, $\frac{1}{6}$ inch wide, on the inside of the frames. The frame front is placed into a hinged, two-part aluminum holding fixture. The fixture is closed, tightly fastened, and pressed against a spinning router blade $\frac{1}{6}$ inch wide. The router can be seen in the left section of the holder.

The fronts are then taken to two machines, each of which grinds down a different area on the inside of the frame. One smoothes the place that rests on the cheek, and the other rounds the edge that touches the nose. The fronts are next taken to an area where the frames are held in a gripping device while a translucent nose pad is glued on. The fronts are left to cure, or dry, for twenty-four hours, after which the nose pad has become a firm and permanent part of the frame. The sections where the pad and frame were glued together are then ground down to create a smooth surface.

In order to connect the temples (the arms that hook around the ears) to the frame fronts, hinges must be attached. At the upper edge of each corner of the frame a small slot, or groove, is cut. Half a metal hinge is put into each slot and the frame front is put into a capitron machine. This device ultrasonically vibrates the metal hinges against the plastic, which produces friction and heat that melt the plastic and cause it to flow around the hinges. This creates a solid bond, which anchors the hinges. Next, the fronts are taken to a plastic printing machine, which applies the name of the company, the style, and the size in small letters on the side of the frames.

For a pair of glasses to fit properly, the temples must be attached to the frame fronts at a tilted angle. To achieve this tilt, the fronts are taken to a small automatic saw, which cuts a compound angle at the two upper edges. Then a small protective cap is fitted over the hinges to prevent them from being damaged during the polishing procedures.

Except for the three areas on the inside of the frames that were ground down after they were stamped out, the fronts are still flat and sharp-edged. To make them smooth, round, and shiny, a series of polishing operations are performed. Several hundred fronts at a time are placed in a rotating barrel in the polishing room. Pumice, a soft stone ground into a powder, is used as a mild abrasive. Maple pegs, one third the size of kitchen matches, are used as the polishing agent. The pegs, which get coated with the pumice in the rotating drum, bang against the frames. This gradual abrasive action slowly smoothes the edges and flat surfaces of the frame fronts. After twenty-four hours of tumbling, the frames are removed from the drum.

The fronts are taken to an oven where they are heated so they are soft and pliable. After being heated, each frame is taken out of the oven and mounted in a form shaped exactly like the fronts but with a slight curve to it, similar to the contour of the face. The mounted frame is placed in a press, which applies pressure for half a minute. This bends the frame so that it acquires the desired curve. The press operator quickly takes the front off the form and dips it into a cold water bath to harden it.

The curved fronts are returned to the polishing room for

These small maple pegs are used to help polish the plastic frames.

The fronts, which have sharp edges, are placed in these drums. Then maple pegs and pumice are added. The drums are rotated for twenty-four hours to smooth all the surfaces of the fronts.

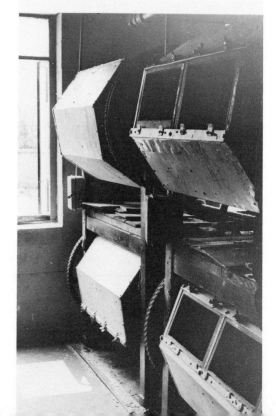

The heated fronts are placed on a curved forming die in a hydraulic press. A block of aluminum with the opposite curve is bolted to the top part of the press. When this block is lowered, the pressure curves the frame front.

the application of a high-finish sheen. They proceed through a series of three tumbling drums for four more days. Two of the drums contain progressively finer pumice, the third, a polishing wax.

The smooth and highly polished fronts are collected after the last tumbling cycle and inspected for any flaws or scratches. They are then placed in envelopes and shelved by size, color, and style.

Most frame manufacturers design and produce a new style every few months to meet the demands of an increasingly popular consumer product. Frame fronts for each style are made in a variety of sizes. There are usually three bridge sizes (the thickness of the upper part of the nose that fits between the nose pads) and three eye sizes (the dimensions of the corrective lenses). As each style is usually made in four colors there can be thirty-six different combinations for each style of frame front.

A hinge, taken from the pile at the lower right, is placed into a groove cut into the arm the worker is holding. They are then both placed in a riveting machine, which forces two rivets through the arms into holes in the hinges. The ends of the rivets are bent over to attach the hinge firmly to the arm.

The temples of the glasses are made in much the same manner as the fronts. Temples are either 5 or 6 inches long and are stamped out from heated sheets of acetate, usually of solid colors that complement the fronts. The temples are then taken to a wire inserting machine, which heats both the temples and a core wire, a narrow strip of steel. When both are at the right temperature, the core wire is forced into the center of the soft plastic temples. All well-made glasses have this reinforcing wire in the temples to insure their strength.

Some temples are flat and angular while others are rounded. Depending on the style, several grinding and shaping operations are performed next. The second half of the hinge is then riveted into a groove cut into the temples. The ends are then cut off to match the angle cut into the

Envelopes marked with the size and color of each front style are placed in boxes on the racks to the right. The different-sized arms are placed in envelopes on the racks in the center. When an order arrives, a worker packages the proper arms and fronts and sends them to the optometrist or optometric supply house.

fronts. After proceeding through a series of polishing operations similar to the treatment the fronts received, the temples are packaged in envelopes by size, color, and style and placed in a stockroom.

Frame manufacturers supply both optometrists and optometric supply houses with sets of frames and temples. Optometrists order the combination of size, color, and style that a customer requires, which is shipped from the factory within twenty-four hours.